EVERY WOMAN KNOWS THIS

A HORROR COLLECTION

BY
LAUREL HIGHTOWER

DEATH KNELL PRESS

EVERY WOMAN KNOWS THIS
A HORROR COLLECTION

Edited by Gabino Iglesias

Cover and interior design by Death Knell Designs
Illustrations by Red Lagoe

ISBN: 979-8-9873397-0-1

Death Knell Press
www.deathknellpress.com

DEATH KNELL PRESS

TABLE OF CONTENTS

ACKNOWLEDGEMENTS

Thanks first to John F.D. Taff, without whose challenge I might never have tried my hand at short stories.

To Professor Brianna Whitten, for teaching one of my stories in her Women's Studies class, a bucket list item for me since I took my own first class in college.

To every editor who found a home for my particular brand of snarky short stories.

To Red Lagoe, who is as fantastic a publisher and artist as she is a friend, which is saying something.

To Gabino Iglesias, for eagle-eyed editing (mixed with plenty of encouragement) that made this a better collection, as well as the generous and confidence-building gift of the first blurb.

To Elle Turpitt, who also edited stories for me before I subbed, and adds that amazing skill to all her others. Thank you, my friend.

To Cina Pelayo, Gemma Amor, and John Langan for graciously agreeing to take time out of their own busy schedules to read and offer blurbs as well. Time is our most precious commodity, and I appreciate it.

To Lilyn George, S.H. Cooper, and Sandra Ruttan for sharp-eyed beta reading, and for your friendship.

To James Sabata, for all the things.

To Anton Cancre, who always brings the party, the heart, and the style.

To the folks at work, for being the right kind of place, and for leaving me head space to do the other things I love. And for telling everyone I write zombie porn. Can't beat that kind of advertising.

To everyone who's ever read, reviewed or suggested my work, whether you liked it or hated it—you spent your time with me, and that's an invaluable gift.

To my horror community—my fellow writers, the reviewers, readers, podcasters, publishers, publicists and everyone in between. Y'all join me on what is otherwise a solitary path and for that I thank you. If I tried to list everyone individually the price of this book would skyrocket, but so long as you know that I know, and I do. Fist bumps, bourbon and blue hearts.

To my horror girls Jessica Clark and Stephanie Woolery, for every laugh, meme and hangout session. To Julia Ritchie for always being there. To Allison Saxton, as amazing a mom as she is a friend and person. To Young-Eun Park, who once lent me laughter when I had none left, and who remains one of my people.

To Chance, Lisa, Mindy, Jenny, Chris and all the booksellers who daily go to bat for horror. You are invaluable, and your efforts are noticed and appreciated.

To Alan and Katie Hightower and Rachel and Wes Ballard, Isaac Fritz, and Everett Ballard. You guys are the best.

To Arthur Wells, a young man I'm daily proud of, and who has taught me much about tolerance, kindness and living in the moment over the last seventeen years.

To David, my partner in love, life, parenting and everything else. You have my past and future.

And as always, to Sebastian. I wished upon a star and got everything I wanted and more. Love you always, Tiny Buddy.

For Sebastian,
because everything I have belongs to you.

And for the women. All women.

EVERY WOMAN KNOWS THIS

There's a certain kind of smile that it's not safe to return—every woman knows this. It's the one from the predator, the anglerfish who shines a light of false friendliness in the darkness of a sea bed you were swimming through just fine on your own. Taken unawares, you didn't even want the bait—not hungry, you hunt your own food, but an ingrained drive you barely understand causes you to smile back before you realize.

Now you're caught. The hook lifts your lips ever higher, a smile you never meant and wish you could take back widening on unwilling lips. You turn away but the anglerfish follows, as does conversation, the next step in this dance. You're only here for liquor, a staple in your diet, and you already know what you want, the neck of the bottle curled in one hand. You don't need the anglerfish's advice, or opinions, and you don't like him getting so close. You hurry through the transaction, wondering for a moment if the clerk will throw you a lifeline, but his eyes are on a different kind of chase. His attention creeps over your shoulder to the woman who works the drive-through window, both ready for the night to end, and he doesn't see the fish swim after you out the door, into the night. The lock clicks in place, the sign turns to closed, and you are alone, staring down a floating Cheshire grin with far too many teeth.

Still polite, but the veneer disintegrating, you wonder if you can swim fast enough for him to get the hint before his temper flares. Anglerfish are known to be volatile so a light fin is needed here. Not enough encouragement to deserve what might happen to you, not enough assertion to bruise the fish's ego, raise his ire. Your halfhearted responses and hunched shoulders should be enough of a visual cue for this fish to fuck off, but that hook is still in your lip, and he's not stopping until he reels you in.

You wish you were a squid, could spurt inky fluid at him that would obscure you from his sight, muddle his concentration, and allow you to escape. Maybe a beta, one of those warriors unafraid of battle. Even a puffer would be good, the ability to blow yourself up, spikes on every surface, not worth the effort it would take to consume you.

But you're none of those things. You're a plain remora, dull-colored, nothing flashy, you hoped to avoid attracting attention. You have no built-in defenses, and your shark is nowhere in sight tonight. It's just you and the predator, so you can't go home. He'll follow you, he'll know where you live, and there will be no peace then until he gets what he wants.

You see this knowledge reflected in his dead, black eyes, and now you're angry. You square your shoulders and tell him to go, you're done with this conversation. His expression goes ugly as you knew it would, gills flaring as he spits out the epithet you've been waiting for.

"Bitch," he says, that smile you never should have returned twisting to a sneer. "You're not too hot for me."

You don't argue, and you hope that means he's done with you. Having recognized you as just another bitch, and his own superiority as a physical specimen, surely he'll swim away in search of more worthy prey. But when you turn to go, he follows. The sound of his pursuit, heavy breathing, a stomping gait, the angry scrape of shoes along asphalt detritus, makes you move faster, even as your body tenses against whatever violence he may choose. He's back there and you can't see him, are vulnerable to his strike that may come at any moment. Your breathing gets fast and ragged, the cold bites at your cheeks, burns your lungs. You think of every story of a missing girl or woman that starts with exactly this dramatization. A hazy figure retreating down a dark street with a looming shadow in pursuit. Will this be your story? Will the liquor store clerk at least tell people you had good taste in whiskey?

At first the anglerfish keeps his distance, like he's trying to be respectful, but he wouldn't know the meaning of the word. He starts talking again, but you don't respond. It's nonsense anyway, garbled sentences about how snotty you are, how all women are like that, how you need to learn your place. He isn't even talking to you, you're just a stand-in for his disappointments. It won't matter who he thinks you are once he lays hands on you—yours is the body that's here, now.

He's talking faster, getting close enough for you to feel his hot breath on your shoulder. Your flesh crawls at the proximity and your mouth goes dry when he starts punctuating every third word with the meaty smack of fist into palm. He's building up to what he wants to do, and you look around the vast, lightless ocean surrounding you. There is no salvation in these waters.

You change direction, veer right, and he doesn't head you off because you're still getting farther away from the lights of safety. You should never have left them, but there was no one around there, either, and you'd hoped you could lose him. There's only one place you can go now.

He swipes at you, fingers brushing your upper arm and you jump away, legs tangling beneath you. You right yourself, manage not to fall, but you're in full flight mode now, and you start to run. Your thighs burn and it doesn't matter how many times you hit the gym a week, the fear is draining you, making you clumsy.

"Get back here, bitch, I just want to talk," he growls, far too close to your ear, and in another lifetime you might stop to try and make him understand everything that's wrong with that sentence. But here it's about survival, and judging the distance left to travel, you know you're not going to make it. The realization almost stops you in your tracks, and then it does, but this time by choice.

You turn, an apology on your face. "Sorry, you're right, I'm being rude."

He hesitates for only seconds before his toothy smile dawns again and he comes closer. "Damn right you are. Now—"

The whiskey bottle comes swinging from the side, connecting with his skull just above his ear. The blow jars your arm up to your shoulder but the glass holds and you peg him again. Don't hit unless you mean it, and if you do, always strike twice.

He goes down, one hand catching your neckline and pulling you down with him, your bra exposed until you work his hand loose. You stand panting above him, hands shaking, glad you bought the good stuff with the thick bottle.

The anglerfish is down, bleeding from his ear, his predatory light dimmed, toothless for the moment. You stare down at him while the blood rushes in your ears, the hook finally worked free from your lip. You can swim away now, but what about tomorrow? What about the next angelfish or sweet blue neon that catches his attention? Will they know not to smile, not to let that hook catch them? You don't like the odds. You look right, in the direction you were headed, and decide to finish the trip.

He's heavy, but you have strong shoulders and you'll get there soon enough. His eyes flutter open at one point and your heart climbs to your throat, but he only slurs a question before closing them again.

"Where're you taking me?"

"To market," you say, letting his head thump over a curb.

When he finally wakes, it's to a susurration of whispers. They circle him in the darkness, darting in and out of sight, and you're watching his eyes when he figures out what they're chanting.

"New fish, new fish, new fish," they say, and you join them.

He struggles to sit up, his eyes unable to focus. "The fuck is this? You bitches better back off." His words are still slurred, he tries to stand and fails.

Crunching gravel signifies the approach of someone new, and the chanting grows louder until a woman with short, white hair and a well-lined face appears in their midst. She carries a big, rough net in her calloused hands, the weight of it braced against her hip. A cigarette dangles from her lower lip, the only flare of light in the darkness. His gaze is drawn to it and he stares, mesmerized, until he sees the gleam of long knives at her side, the blood-covered apron that hangs to her knees.

"New fish?" she asks, her voice a comforting rasp.

"New fish," the unseen circle confirms.

"The fuck are you?" asks the anglerfish, the smile nowhere in sight.

The old woman leans over and smiles her own lure, throws the net over his thrashing body. "Who am I?" she returns, but it's for the crowd to answer, a laugh rippling through them.

"She's the fishmonger," you say, but his expression says he doesn't get it. He will. The fishmonger is where you bring a catch like him to be cleaned and deboned, strung up for sale next to the other fresh seafood. The fishmonger and her school know the circling currents of the predators; the anglers, the barracuda, the eels with their dull eyes and sharp teeth. They have learned there is strength in numbers, and in knives, and they are always here when they're needed.

Every woman knows this.

THE DANCE

There was magic in Christmas. Not just the kind that delighted children as they stared up at a frozen night sky, hoping for a sight of something that twinkled closer than the stars. Greg was forty-one years old, but he'd never lost the magic of the season. He felt it in the deepest parts of himself—the way the year winnowed down to this small, hushed place. A low burning flame that could light the way for anything—anything at all. Christmas Eve, when the world held its frozen breath and listened.

Greg was listening now. It was one of the things Judy had once loved about him, before everything changed and his belief became a burden. Though they'd never had children, and didn't particularly want them, Greg brought all the joy of Christmas on his own. He insisted on staying up late on Christmas Eve, letting the clock pass midnight. That was the truest time of magic, he would tell her, his face lit only by the warm lights of the tree. He thought she loved him best in those moments. Her lips curled and the smile found her eyes, and she'd reach for his hand and watch his face, letting his joy infect her. It had always been their time, their special magic, and he missed those days. He missed them like hell.

Which was why he was here, again, hoping for another chance, though she'd told him not to. Warned was more like it, her anger growing each time he ignored her wishes. He knew he shouldn't keep trying, that she was gone and wasn't coming back. That wasn't why he was doing this. There was no getting his wife back, and he accepted that, but what he couldn't accept was the loss of their special magic together. She felt it too, every time. It just didn't bring her smile the way it used to.

He turned the lights down in the den, where they always placed their tree. Some of the ornaments they'd bought together, the ones from their earliest and brokest days, were tattered and wilted. The warm white lights still glowed, as he painstakingly replaced each bulb when it burned out. He wasn't sure what part each piece played in the ritual, but he didn't want to risk losing his chance.

A fire burned in the old wood stove, but low, the cold creeping into the dark corners of the room. *It's a Wonderful Life* played mutely on the big screen behind him, and Judy's favorite Christmas album crackled and skipped through the speakers. Greg took a breath and held it until he felt what he'd been waiting for. A lowering of the temperature, a thinning of the air. He smoothed his shirt and pressed close to the front window, his gaze on the cloudless, ebony sky, and he wished. He thought one of the stars winked, flashed a brighter light, and then was gone.

He smelled her before he heard her. The stench was bad this time, worse than the last. He'd thought the smell would get better over time, but a thick odor of rot coated his tongue as soon as he breathed it in.

"You promised."

Greg turned, and she was there. Standing by the fireplace, her back to him, the rigid set of her shoulders a reminder that he would need to tread lightly.

"I'm sorry," he said, the tremor in his voice genuine and meant to ward off her reaction.

She sighed and the smell grew worse, a sulfurous stench carried from her rotting lungs. She sounded like she was going to cry, and her shoulders slumped beneath her soil-spattered sweater. "I'm so tired, Greg. So very, very tired."

He tried not to hear the edge to her voice, the note that was next door to a growl. The way that something much darker than Judy had ever been scratched its way to the surface. He never asked the nature of the magic that brought them together each Christmas. It wouldn't have mattered— these brief moments together were worth everything.

"Merry Christmas, babe," he said, and took a step toward her, arms outstretched.

She tensed again, and still did not turn. "Stay away."

"Judy, please. It doesn't matter to me—I love you as you are."

She gave a broken sob that seemed to come from many throats. "You don't know what I am, anymore. If you did you wouldn't keep making this wish." She turned her head just enough for him to see her shadowed profile. The tendons of her jaw and the rotting teeth within were visible through the flesh that had faded since last year. Her eye was a strange, bright green. Like a single, unblinking Christmas light, he thought.

"Judy, please. It isn't so much to ask, is it? Just one dance. Like we used to."

She said nothing but her shadowed fingers flexed, claw-like, in the flickering fire light.

He put his hands on her cold shoulders, ignoring the

protruding bone beneath. "One dance to keep the magic alive. Please."

As the first notes of *Greensleeves* sounded from the speakers, she turned in his hold. Her face, mostly skeletal but for that one green eye, the other socket gaping and empty, was as beautiful to him as the day she'd died. She let him wrap his arms around her and sway with the music, feeling the magic flow through his every cell. He knew, as she tucked her head beneath his chin, and he felt the graze of her teeth at his throat, that this might be the last time. They were growing older, and things never stayed the same. That was okay. The magic of Christmas would endure.

THE BRIDE WORE BLACK

Despite the seventeen recorded deaths that had taken place in Helmhurst's long history, the sprawling mansion wasn't haunted. Not in the traditional sense, which had always been a source of disappointment for Claudia. Both when she'd visited, many years ago as a young girl, and now, a respected matron and property owner of forty-two summers. It might have been expected that she would grow out of that childish fixation; a thrill of anticipation as she climbed those steep stone steps, a creeping dread as the huge wooden doors creaked open before her. Even the obvious neglect of the past decade only added to her enjoyment—all the furniture draped in dusty white sheets, cobwebs fluttering from every corner of the high ceilings, and the musty scent of abandonment. The estate, built in the grand times when many generations lived under the same roof, was far too large for modern convenience, and now lingered in trust, awaiting someone to take responsibility for it. No one had lived here for quite some time, and there had been ample opportunity for any specters to stake their claim.

Still, no matter where she searched, no matter what dark stories of the manor's past she dug up, Claudia never saw a ghost. And though both her grandfather and her aunt had died behind these walls in the meantime, she didn't expect that to change today. No, Claudia was after something more tangible on her first trip back to Helmhurst since her grandfather's wake.

A book. *The* book. The one her parents had all but convinced her didn't exist. She'd been seven when she last saw it; easy to remember, since it was the year of the fire. A blocked chimney flue that contributed five deaths to Helmhurst's impressive total. Claudia felt the same shrinking guilt she always did when she remembered the fire, the way the bodies of the servants looked as they were pulled from the smoke-scorched attic. It had been thirty-five years, and as an adult, she knew it hadn't been her fault, not really. She could look into the past and forgive a frightened seven-year-old who didn't understand what she'd seen. It didn't stop that cringing pain, the certainty that the tragedy could have been prevented. The book had shown her the way. Maybe it could again.

"I know you're here," Claudia said to the empty house, in a soft tone without echo. There was no response, but she felt a quickening in the atmosphere, and smiled. It wanted to be found.

It didn't take her long to get settled. The grocer had delivered the food she'd ordered, and the necessary rooms had been made ready for her. The kitchen, bathroom, and her childhood room of old. The rest of the fifteen or so bedrooms and numerous parlors had been left alone, a long, dingy gauntlet of closed doors to her right and left as she made her way down the second floor hallway. She was tempted to open those doors, explore every nook and cranny of the grand old place. Wood paneled rooms, thick green carpet, hideous silk wallpaper no doubt peeling from the plaster beneath. Who knew what forgotten treasures lurked under draped covers? But she didn't want the distraction. She was itching to get her search underway, feeling an urgency that wasn't merited by the circumstances. She had plenty of time. Three days until George arrived with the rest of their wedding entourage. Three days before a host of family, friends, cooks, bakers, florists, and who knew who else descended and destroyed the peace of Helmhurst. All in the name of marital bliss. A shiver of unease made her shoulders hunch, and she frowned without knowing it. She loved George. She should be happy. She *was* happy. She just had to check this one last thing.

Lit candelabra in hand, Claudia slowly climbed the grand staircase, her hand sliding up the banister and disturbing decades-worth of grime, until she stood outside the door she'd been dreaming about for months. It was massive, at least twice as tall as she, made of mahogany and ornately carved with storybook scenes. Some she recognized, others she didn't. One or two that looked downright sinister, like the one in the lower right. A fork-tongued creature with curling ram's horns and the lower body of a goat held something concealed in both clawed hands, offering it to a figure in a cloak. She gave a delicious shiver and reached for the heavy handle, pushing her way inside the library.

It was as magical inside as it had been in her dreams. Two full stories of shelves, packed with books of every appearance and subject. Oil paintings depicting yet more literary scenes hung in the few places where shelves had not been crammed, and here and there strange artifacts from her great-grandfather's travels acted as book ends. The ceiling was high and sweeping, moonlight admitted by a small skylight high above. Claudia knew that George would love this room, and this time the thought of her fiancé brought a smile to her face. The only person in her life who read as much as she did, and the only one who didn't chastise her for the amount of time she spent with her nose in a book. They'd met at a lending library, in fact, and their shared love of reading had put the first cracks in her armament.

She went to the cluster of covered furniture in the middle of the room. She didn't lift the cloth, but could picture the intimidating leather couch and matching set of chairs that waited beneath. The fireplace was dark and cold, the room itself an impenetrable black. The air in here was dry and chill, and underlying the stale scent of disuse was the heady smell of leather-bound books. She breathed deep and thought of how to start. There were no gaslights, but there were plenty of candles, so she lit as many as she could find, the brittle wicks flaming large as accumulated dust combusted from each one. Soon the library was lit in a soft glow, enough for her to make out the shelves that lined the wall.

Her heart sunk. There had to be thousands of books here, all of them coated in thick layers of dust, and she had no idea what she was looking for. A swift inventory indicated her grandfather had organized his shelves by subject, and alphabetical by author within each of those. But the book had no title, no author, and Claudia didn't know how anyone would have classified its genre. The subject matter was *her*.

She knew that now, all these years later. That the little girl depicted in the pages of the enchanting book was, if not Claudia exactly, a twin or shadow of hers. Although if it were a shadow, it was one that cast into the future.

Not at the beginning, of course. When she'd first paged through the odd little book, what mesmerized her was the depiction of another little girl, close in age to Claudia herself. By that time the remaining extended family had dwindled, some lost at war, others moving off to begin a new life far from the mansion's checkered past. Claudia had no brothers or sisters, no cousins close in age and living nearby, visiting Helmhurst at the same time, ready made friends. Instead, she'd spent those long visits roaming empty, echoing halls by herself, reading in forgotten nooks, or acting out complicated scenes in the garden.

It was a day in the garden she'd seen depicted, when she'd flipped to the first page. A garden similar to, but not exactly like Helmhurst's. And the girl, with two braids instead of one, and a green dress instead of Claudia's blue. But the scene was the same—Claudia the lion tamer, head of the traveling circus. A stick in one hand for fending off the beast, and the other empty, curled around the hilt of a make-believe whip.

Claudia had clapped her hands in delight, thrilled at this small connection. It made her feel seen, and not so alone. Her elation dimmed when she turned the page to find it blank, and all the subsequent ones as well. She'd been disappointed, hoping to see more pictures of the little girl, but she soon abandoned the book and returned to her solitary play.

The next time she saw the book, it was sitting on the arm of the reading chair she preferred. Drawn to the promise of seeing the little girl again, she flipped it open, and this time there was an illustration on the second page. The same girl in a different dress, with four buttons instead of Claudia's six, but she stood on a stool in a kitchen much like Helmhurst's, kneading dough at the instruction of a woman in servant's garb. Claudia tilted her head, studying the page. The woman didn't look like Miss Ellie, the housekeeper she'd known from her earliest days, but there was a familiarity depicted between the two figures that made her believe they shared a similar relationship. And that was precisely what Claudia had spent her morning doing—learning to make bread.

The picture hadn't been there the last time she'd looked; she'd been sure of that. This kitchen scene was new, had appeared in the weeks since she'd opened the book. She flipped back to the first drawing, only to find it gone. There was the page it had been on, the very first, but now it was as blank as all the others, except the second. How had it happened? She might have believed that someone in the household with a hidden artistic talent had drawn another picture to add to the first. But going to the trouble of removing the first page, and replacing it with a blank one? She ran her fingers over the inner binding, finding no razored edges or telltale glue. She held the paper up to the light, wondering if perhaps a chemical mixture of some kind had been used to dissolve the image. Her father had shown her once how to use lemon juice as an invisible ink, but the paper was high quality, creamy white, and blank as new snow.

She flipped to the cover, wondering who had authored this curiosity, but there were no words there, either. No title, no credit. At the age of seven, Claudia knew nothing of copyright or editions, but all the other books she'd read had a page dedicated to naming the publisher and other boring information she always skipped over. This book was entirely blank, except for the single drawing.

It was a scintillating mystery, and one Claudia determined to keep to herself. Adults were strange creatures, often scandalized by things that seemed perfectly natural to her. Almost everything she did was a violation of some unwritten social contract, so she wasn't about to disclose her secret book and have it taken away from her. She wasn't allowed to remove books from the library, so she found a hiding place for it, tucked in the space behind a shelf of books about archaeology.

Ever after that, Claudia visited the book each day. And each day, a new page would appear, showing the little girl taking part in the same activity Claudia had, earlier in the day. They were never identical, nor were the settings, but close enough that she felt a strong kinship to the girl.

She usually visited in the early afternoon, after lunch when everyone else was having a lie-down. It was her special time alone in the house, and now she devoted it to the book. But one morning, she decided to see what would happen if she went early, before any of the day's activities took place. Would the page from the previous day still be there, awaiting her next exploit before updating? Would all the pages be blank? Or would it show the little girl sleeping, or cleaning her teeth, from lack of better choices?

To her surprise, she found the next page had already been filled, with a scene of the girl having a picnic under a tree, her hair wet, laughing as she pressed against the trunk to avoid the worst of the rain shower that must have surprised her. Claudia studied the picture, wondering why this scene. She hadn't planned a picnic, had in fact, avoided making plans so she could see what the book would do. But now it seemed the perfect activity for the morning. The day was lovely, not a cloud in sight, and Claudia couldn't think of anything she'd rather do. So she packed up her breakfast in a basket and wandered until she found the best place to eat. She was looking for the tree, the one the girl had sought shelter under, but didn't see a perfect match, and so settled on the one that provided the best canopy. She was glad she had when, despite there being not the slightest hint of rain, a storm blew up from nowhere. She abandoned her sodden breakfast and pressed herself against the tree's trunk, laughing as she watched the shower, and wondering how the book had known.

That was it, she decided later that day, when she'd crept back to the library to look again. The day's picture was unchanged, still the laughing little girl caught in a rainstorm. The book had somehow known what Claudia would do that day, before she herself did. She pondered this, wondering if she would have chosen to have a picnic if the book hadn't given her the idea, but there was no escaping the fact that the book had predicted the rain.

It was an enjoyable novelty for a time after that, letting the book decide what she would do that day, or warn her of inclement weather. It was never wrong, but as blank pages piled up behind the daily illustration, the predictions reached further into the future. Once it showed the arrival of a tall, elegant woman, sweeping up the lane in a glossy carriage drawn by four matched grays. The book girl rushed to meet her and Claudia waited all day, and the next, before her Aunt Teresa arrived the afternoon of the third day.

"What took you so long?" she demanded as her favorite aunt pulled her into an embrace and kissed her cheek.

Aunt Teresa smiled down at her. "Whatever can you be speaking of, Claudia? I only decided this morning to pay a surprise visit."

Claudia closed her lips as she realized the implication of her aunt's words. The book had known before Teresa herself had, and unlike the rained out picnic, it could not be a result of suggestion or influence. It was truly foretelling the future. Somehow, with another person being involved, it made it more real. And was that any more fantastic than the appearance and disappearance of the pages each day?

As time went on, the scenes the book depicted began to stretch ever farther into the future. A few days, to a week, to two. Claudia found herself wondering as she studied those pages in pleasant anticipation—was the book indeed *telling* the future, or was it somehow bringing these events into being? She had always felt a kinship with the girl depicted there—was she somehow responsible for these little alleviations of Claudia's lonely routine?

The stories told by the book were nearly always enjoyable, but one morning it presented Claudia with a scene that frightened her. She opened to the newest page and drew back, faced with a depiction of fire. Black smoke filled the edges of the drawing, and she could almost smell it. She slammed the book closed and refused to visit for several days. When she opened it again, the page had not changed, but the picture had. The fire was worse, with more detail, showing a bedroom door and low ceilings. She slammed it closed again, but for the next eight days, the picture expanded, showing more details of the fire to come. Claudia was frightened, on edge, spending her time peering around corners and keeping a wary eye on the kitchen and many fireplaces Helmhurst was so well-provided with. One in nearly every room—far too many opportunities for errant embers or flying sparks.

When disaster struck, it was in the servants' quarters, a fortnight after the book first warned of fire. She stood at the base of the attic stairs, tears streaming down her face, crying for Miss Ellie, but the housekeeper had been lost to the tragedy, suffocated by smoke when a blocked chimney caught fire.

Claudia was inconsolable. Why hadn't she told anyone what the book had warned her about? Could she have prevented those five deaths if she had only shared what she knew? She stayed away from the book for a week, and when she finally returned, tears dripping from her nose to the pages beneath, the picture waiting her was unlike any she had seen before.

The girl sat on the floor with her legs crossed, just as Claudia did. She stared through the page at Claudia, her eyes sad, mouth a straight line. Was there disappointment there? It seemed there was, and Claudia was overcome with guilt once again.

"I'm sorry," she whispered to the little girl. "I wish I'd done something. It's my fault they're dead, isn't it?"

The girl didn't answer, and her expression never changed, but Claudia knew the truth. After that day, the picture never changed again. She became obsessed with it, returning many times a day to sit and stare at the girl, beg her forgiveness, ask for another chance. She felt as though her only friend had abandoned her, and on top of losing Miss Ellie, it was too much for a child to bear.

As was inevitable, the book was discovered by Claudia's mother. Worried at her daughter's drooping mien and continued silence, she followed the child and found her with the book. It seemed she was angry even before she forced an explanation from Claudia, her nostrils flaring when she saw the book open on the floor, snatching it up and slamming it shut.

"Where did you find this?" she hissed, yanking Claudia up by one wrist.

Claudia's surprise at her mother's treatment was dulled by guilt. She felt that her mother's ire was earned. She had, after all, caused the deaths of five people in the attic above, while the family of Helmhurst slept below. She expected punishment, possibly banishment, but the only consequence was the loss of the book. After that day, Claudia never saw it again, no matter how hard she looked. When she asked, her parents denied all knowledge, and over time she accepted their version of the truth with relief. If there had been no book, then there was no guilt. There was only tragic, unpreventable death.

Now, however, Claudia knew better. Her memories of the book, of the little girl, had grown sharper in the last weeks. Her dreams were vivid, inhabited by that little girl grown. She'd woken three mornings ago with the certainty that this was something she needed to do, before she could fully commit to the new life she had chosen. The book would show her if she were making a mistake; she was sure of it. She told herself she expected to open to a page showing her happy future with George; a joyous wedding day, long afternoons spent reading side by side, traveling and sight-seeing without the onerous restrictions of being a woman on her own. George was perfect for her, they were compatible in every way. She didn't *need* the book to tell her what she already knew, but she wanted it.

Claudia hunted long into the night, each shelf subjected to a search in the cavities behind the rows of properly shelved books, each one turning up empty. She studied spines, but so many lacked notations, and she couldn't remember the size or the color of the tome. She sat on the floor and looked around her, wondering how to narrow the search. There were thousands of books. Would she need to open all of them?

As she made her way to her room in the small hours of the morning, Claudia tried not to feel discouraged. Already beginning the ticklish task of undressing without assistance, she unlaced her overdress and ran her hands along the corset beneath. Then she froze, sense memory stirred.

Black lace binding. That was it; that was how she would find it. She couldn't recall how the book looked, but she knew how it felt beneath her fingers—black lace binding over a silken cover. She raced back up the grand stairs to the library half-dressed. The candles guttered in their sockets, but she had no need for light. She closed her eyes and began a slow tour of the shelves, tracing the spines of each book. It took two trips around before her fingertips snagged on delicate lace.

Her breath caught; she opened her eyes and looked at the treasure she had pulled from the shelves. This was it: the book.

Trembling, she sat on the floor by the largest candelabra, legs folded in unconscious imitation of her younger self. She opened the book with shaking hands, and flipped through empty pages. On and on she turned, each one as empty as the last, and she began to panic, knowing she was nearing the end. Would it still work for her? Was the little girl there at all?

The image that finally appeared made Claudia drop the book, hands covering her mouth. It fell open to the same page and a face stared out at her, but not the face of the girl. Or, at least, not the one she was expecting. It was Sarah, the youngest servant lost in the fire all those years ago. She couldn't have been more than fourteen at the time, and the eyes fixed on Claudia's through the distance of the page were haunted and hollow. Her clothes were scorched, the flesh of her face red and tightened. Claudia began to hyperventilate, her hands shaking as she reached out to turn the page.

For the first time ever, there was a second page illustrated, but it brought no relief from the first. There were Jed and Alec, two of the stable hands who usually slept in the hayloft, but who had been brought inside on that frigid night by the agency of Ms. Ellie's warm heart. They, too, had perished, and now they stared out at Claudia with twin haunted expressions. Tears squeezed from her eyes, and she turned the page, knowing what she would find.

Ms. Ellie herself, standing behind old Cook, who's eyes, red and bloodshot, bulged from her face. Claudia gave a scream, leaned away, but Ms. Ellie's eyes seemed to follow her.

"I'm sorry," she whispered, tears spilling freely now. "I'm sorry I never told anyone. I'm sorry I didn't warn you. I'm sorry I killed you."

There was no answer, and no change in those empty visages. With no forgiveness forthcoming, Claudia reached out to turn the page once more, and she was there; the girl, though she was a girl no longer, anymore than Claudia was. She had aged as well, her long hair down around her shoulders, her own dress half-buttoned. Much as she had in the last picture Claudia had been shown, the woman sat and stared at her.

"Are you still angry with me?" Claudia asked in a whisper, wiping at her eyes with the back of her hand.

She blinked, and the picture changed. The woman now frowned at her, though Claudia hadn't turned the page. Her breath coming quick, she blinked, and the woman sat up straighter.

Claudia did as well. "You once warned me of disaster before it struck. I did not listen, and I have regretted it my life long. You owe me nothing, but I wish to ask, once more."

In the next blink, the woman's eyes grew wide. In the one after that she leaned, as though she were peering at something behind Claudia. In the stop motion of a moving picture, Claudia saw the woman become alarmed, then gesture, then finally lift the candelabra next to her in a threatening fashion. Claudia cringed away, certain the woman would attack her somehow, when she heard a creak behind her, and a gust of air made the candles flicker.

Heart pounding, she gripped the heavy candelabra beside her and turned.

"George?" she said, confused to see her intended husband looming beside her in the darkness.

"Claudia? What on earth are you doing here in the dark,

my love?"

Claudia choked on a sob and stood, falling into his arms. The terror that had held her spellbound since finding the book had finally broken, and she felt the quivering relief through her whole body. He held her close, one hand stroking her hair, murmuring something unintelligible and comforting.

She drew back and looked up into his homely, familiar face. "What are you doing here? I wasn't expecting you until Tuesday."

He put a hand to her face, and she remembered the state she was in.

"I wanted to surprise you—to have some time to ourselves before the circus begins." He smiled down at her. "Was that all right?"

Claudia stepped back to pull her dress closed, sniffed back the residue of her tears. "Yes, of course it's all right. I'm glad to see you." And she was, though there was still a flare of annoyance that she wasn't to have her last days of solitude. Still, it was good he had come—Claudia shuddered to think of sleeping here alone, after what she had seen in the book.

George clasped her hand, his gaze rising to take in what he could of the room in the uncertain light. "Good heavens, is this the library you told me about? It's magnificent."

She smiled as he moved toward the shelves, his hand tugging hers, but she pulled him back. "Not tonight. I know you, you'll get lost in contemplation and we'll never get to bed. Come now, it's late."

He turned to her with a raised eyebrow. "Does that mean we're sharing a bed tonight? Before the wedding? Scandalous, my dear."

She swatted at him. It wouldn't be the first time they had slept together. Though it certainly wasn't conventional, Claudia was forty-two years old and independent. She did what she damn well pleased in the city, and there was no one here to judge them. "We have the place to ourselves for now. We can do as we wish."

George went to gather his things, and her gaze strayed to the book, where it sat closed on the floor by the window. On impulse, she ran and collected it, tucking it beneath her arm before leading the way to her bedroom. After all, George was here now, and she had no reason to be frightened. What was more, she didn't think she would sleep that night until she resolved the mystery of what the book wanted to tell her.

Later, as she combed out her hair before joining George in bed, she looked to the chair where she had left the book. He was reading, after all, and wouldn't think it was strange of her to do so as well. She clutched it to her nightdress and slid beneath the warm, ornate duvet. George leaned over to kiss her before returning to his book, and she settled in, apprehension making her heart beat fast.

She held her breath, and opened the book. Its pages fell to both sides, revealing a single illustration taking up both pages, and her jaw dropped as she took it in.

It was George. George at Helmhurst, in the library, and they were together, as she had pictured them, though never like this. George lay prone in front of the great fireplace, legs twisted, an arm positioned as though wrenched from its socket. His head was a mass of blood, bone, and pulped flesh, crimson shining from the page, and she knew if she touched it, the paint would be smooth, slick, satin finished.

"Claudia, dear?"

George's voice made her jump, her heart pounding. She looked over at him, expecting to see his beaten body, but it was only him. Comfortable, safe, familiar George.

"Is everything all right, sweetheart? You look as though you'd seen a ghost."

Claudia found no words to answer him, looking again at the drawing, hoping she had been mistaken. But there was no change—poor George still lay in a pool of blood on the library floor. And standing over him, a heavy candelabra clutched in one hand, blood and hair clinging to one side, crimson spatter adorning her gown and splashed across her face, was Claudia herself.

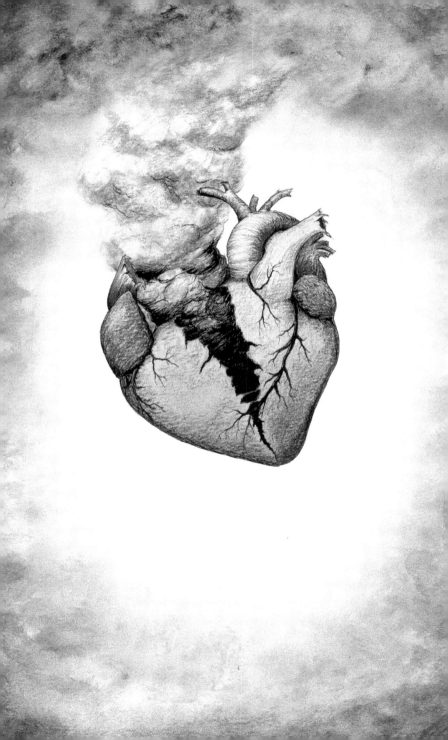

VIGNETTES OF WOMANHOOD

SCAR TISSUE

Three a.m. watches when she thought the worry was done. Eyes closed, not staring at the ceiling, that would admit defeat. Bullets dodged, fifty caliber, and wondering when their number will come up. Scar tissue, maybe, but his father died of lung cancer last year and no one knew until it was far too late. *Do you have a family history of cancer?* they ask, and before he can finish listing the occasions of cells gone mad they stop him, because the answer is yes. How many times can one family dance with death? Exhaustion, and the rush of fear, the knowledge of alone. What the fuck. *How* the fuck. Knowing everyone has a cross to bear, but Jesus, don't let this be his.

Riding down the elevator from the oncology floor that bloody fucking week in the gray time of not knowing. The woman with the IV stand, sad smile and squeezed hand to the man that rides with her.

"I'm sorry," the woman says. "For everything this is putting on you."

He declaims, and she sees her future in their lives. Or not. It's for someone else to say, but for fuck's sake, at least he's still ornery enough to drive the nurses crazy.

"You married him," snorts one, only halfway joking.

"I know," she thinks, among other things.

THE MIDWIFE

Sentries stood at the outskirts of the settlement, eyes squinting into the lightlessness beyond. Torchlight flickered, chasing shadows, then bringing them back again. Two men stood shoulder to shoulder, watching the treeline.

"Will she come?" asked the younger man, his beard a mere suggestion of shadow.

"She'll come," the older man confirmed, fingers tightening around the stock of his weapon. He glanced down at his companion. "Don't fret, Adam. You always worry more with your own."

His young friend scowled into the night. "But you said she always comes. How does she know?"

The other man grunted. "Don't matter how she knows, she just does. She's the Midwife. She'll be here."

Both men cringed when a scream broke the quiet. They didn't need to look at each other to know their hearts were racing.

"Wish she wouldn't do that," muttered Adam, his shoulders straightening as he resumed his watch.

"You can hardly blame her," chuckled his friend. "Hurts like the devil, or so my Bonnie tells me at least once a day."

"Still, though. Don't they teach 'em, nowadays? How to get through without the drugs and all? Better for everyone that way, isn't it?"

The man's heavy face was set in a frown. "Midwife'll take care of that, anyway."

Tracy bit back a groan as the contraction seized her. She knew Lyla wouldn't judge her, but she didn't want to seem like a wuss. Not when her sister had already been through it three times. She rode the wave, counting, and breathed out when it let go.

Lyla smiled at her. "Better?"

Tracy nodded. She cast a glance around the dimly lit, single-room dwelling she and her husband called home. The baby would have a small place set aside in the far corner. Tracy's eyes strained to penetrate the shadows there, wondering if that was where it would come from. Where *she* would come from.

"You're worrying again," said Lyla. "Don't. It's the last thing you need to be thinking about right now."

Tracy looked at her sister, away from the impenetrable blackness. "I can't help it. I don't want her to come. She scares the hell out of me."

Lyla patted her arm, then moved a pillow behind her sister's back. "I know. It's not as bad as you're making it out to be, though. And it's not like we have a choice."

Tracy gritted her teeth against another cramping wave, waiting it out before she spoke again. "How can it not be bad? She comes to steal from us, on what should be the happiest day of our lives."

Lyla shook her head. "Only the cries. That's all the Midwife wants."

Tracy shuddered at her sister's mention of the name. "Just mine? Or the baby's, too?"

Her sister looked down at her lap. "It depends."

"On what?"

"If you have a boy or a girl."

Tears started to Tracy's eyes. She wanted a girl—always had, ever since she was little. But knowing what it would cost the child, she couldn't wish for it. And this theft would only be the first of many. She hated the unfairness of it all. "How can you tell me not to be afraid of that?" she asked. "She's not even *human*."

Lyla shrugged and took her sister's hand. "A lot of things aren't. Haven't been for a while." Both women's eyes strayed to the bolted front door, to the darkness beyond it. "At least it's better than having the others come, too. You want that again?"

Tracy shuddered, breathed through more pain. "No. But it shouldn't have to be a choice. And I don't even get to have Adam here—he should be here."

Her sister raised an eyebrow. "You think he'd be much use?"

Tracy gave a tired laugh, because she knew that's what Lyla was aiming for. "Maybe not. But it's just sad. I feel like we're being robbed of a lot more than a cry."

Even that was enough to make her shudder, a hand of ice closing over her spine. How could someone's cry be stolen, anyway? It didn't make sense. Would her voice be gone forever, once the Midwife came? Except that didn't make sense, since Lyla still had hers. So did all three of Lyla's children. Whatever the creature did, it didn't cause permanent damage.

"How does she do it?" Tracy asked in a whisper as the night drew to its deepest point.

Lyla stared into the fire. "I don't know."

"Don't you remember?"

Tracy saw her sister's shoulders tighten. "I remember. Every time, I remember. I just don't know how it's done."

"Does it hurt?" she asked in a small voice.

Lyla smiled at her. "You think you'll notice, with everything else going on?"

That didn't make her feel better. She wondered if her sister was trying to protect her from the truth. Because how could it not hurt? To have your cries stolen right from your own throat. And to think of the same thing happening to a tiny baby, a helpless infant. Tears gathered, fell to either side of her swollen face as she lay her head back. She closed her eyes and let them come. Fuck bravery. She was giving birth, with no anesthetic, and no one but her sister to help her. She'd scream if she damn well wanted to.

Except the noise frightened her. Was that what drew the Midwife? What if she managed to remain silent throughout? Would the thing stay away? She wanted that more than anything, to keep the cruel and sneaking creature from this moment. But how could a person stop a child's cry? You couldn't, and Tracy wouldn't subject her baby to something she was too scared to experience herself.

She wanted Adam. He might not have been useful from a medical standpoint, but he could hold her hand, keep her safe from the Midwife. But that was part of the bargain as well. The Midwife didn't like men, wouldn't have them there when she came creeping around on her dirty errands. So the women were alone, with the birth, and with the unnatural creature who came for their cries.

It consumed her thoughts, overwhelmed the pain at times even as the contractions grew worse. But when a vice of agony closed on her lower back, adding its voice to the excruciating harmony and never letting up, all thoughts of the Midwife left her. She only cared about making it stop. Fuck moaning through it, as she'd been taught. Tracy began to scream, and whatever her sister might have said in comfort or in warning was lost to the roar in her ears.

Then she saw it. A deeper shadow, like polished onyx, skittering around the farthest edges of the light. The door hadn't opened, but it was inside none the less. The Midwife had come to collect.

Tracy panted, her eyes wide as she followed the creature's movements around the room. She looked at her sister, but couldn't tell what Lyla saw, if anything. *Is this part of it?* she thought in panic. Was she supposed to ignore it, the chitinous body clicking and slithering through the shadows? It was coming for her, creeping closer. She struggled to find it, to pin down where it was so it couldn't take her by surprise, but she couldn't do it. Her eyes lost it each time, and the agony rolled through her in an endless wave.

She gave up, thinking that perhaps the Midwife would kill her, and end this pain. Her world narrowed to that fine point, of wanting it to end and nothing else. Whatever it took. She begged her sister to kill her, and she meant it. The baby meant nothing, it was an abstract concept compared to this.

As her suffering crescendoed, Tracy threw her head back to scream but stopped when she felt something slither through her sweat soaked hair. It crept up her neck, probing her ear, then crawled over her open mouth. Spidery fingers spread her dry, cracked lips.

Tracy screamed, then gagged as the fingers slid inside her mouth and down her throat. Her silenced cry hung heavy in the hot, smoky room, its echoes dying in her ears. She tried to scream again but it was cut off—a strange sensation, but not painful. Especially not compared to how the rest of her body felt.

With her voice silenced, Tracy was again able to hear Lyla.

"Push, babe, you've almost got it! One more good one and you're done. You can do it, I promise."

She listened to her older sister, as she always had, and seconds later heard the baby's cries. The sound jolted tears to her eyes, happy ones this time, as love washed over her. When the infant's voice ceased she felt bereft.

"It's a girl," said Lyla, her voice shaking.

"Give her to me," Tracy sobbed, relieved to find her voice returned. As Lyla handed her daughter to her, filament-thin appendages retreated from the child, accompanied by a dry, rustling skitter. Tracy watched the shadows as the creature slid to the front door and into the night. Gone—for now. She shuddered as she held her baby close to her chest, both of them weeping in silence.

The Midwife scuttled through the night, keeping to the most shadowed parts of the forest, clutching the bottle to the carapace of her chest. Its glow was a subtle, shining blue, and it lit her way, not that she needed it. She'd been part of this world for a long time, both before and after the changes. She had simply changed with it, though not of her own choice. It was a truth that had once made her angry, rebellious. As resentful as that young thing giving birth tonight. Wanting things to go back to the way they were, when life was more fair.

Except it wasn't fair, and never had been. She remembered enough of that distant, hazy time before to know that. The coming of the dark, of the creatures of the night, had only created new struggles, new inequities. The Midwife was one of them, and she knew it. Had almost ceased to be bothered by it.

She looked up into a moonless, starless sky. It would stay this way, perfect, velvet nightfall, until she was ready. She needed the time tonight to do her work. The baby had come just when it was needed, for her materials had run low, and the night was pressing closer than she liked. She hurried, willing the many legs that were part of this new form to get her there in time.

A cry split the silence. It was one of Them, and it was close. Her instinct was to freeze, to rid herself of the bottle with the soft blue glow that was doubtless the reason it was searching for her. That, or the scent of the humans she'd been with so recently. It stirred their hunger, which had grown rampant of late. She'd noticed signs that they had turned on each other—a ragged set of bones, the meat picked almost clean. Good, she'd thought with venom. Let them destroy each other.

Another cry, closer than before. A minute later it was answered by one to her right. Her many eyes narrowed. They were tracking her. They knew her errand.

Still, as close as they were, she'd thought she was safe, that she would make it in time. Until a low pitched clicking issued from the shadows just behind her, deep enough to resonate in her bones. Her breath froze in her chest, her movement arrested. If one was that close, there were more, many more she couldn't see. Wouldn't want to, even if she could. However much horror her own visage conjured in the women she visited, she knew it was nothing to the twisted vision of these night things.

She heard the pounding of feet somewhere up ahead, the leathery flap of their wings, smelled their fetid breath. Sensed movement in the darkness as they flanked her. This close, they didn't need to scream anymore, communicating instead in those low clicks and whirs. She looked down at the precious bottle tucked close, secured by many fingers.

Shadows parted beside her, and she saw the first twisted, clawed, appendage feel its way into the moonlight. The Midwife stared at the unnatural sheen of that ragged claw and pictured it piercing her body. She lurched into motion again, put on a burst of speed but was brought up short seconds later. Excruciating pain exploded as reality caught up to her imagination, those claws digging deep on all sides. She felt the popping give of the outer shell of her flesh, the sting and ooze of her innards sliding out. She screamed as they dragged her back, and the one that had tracked her, been behind her the whole time, came lurching into view.

Eyes. So many eyes, glowing red, in places where eyes had no business being. She felt seen, all too exposed to the gaze of hunger personified. It leaned in close and there was little else she could see beyond all those eyes, a precursor to the teeth that would come. Its mouth opened, something like a sharpened tusk protruded, and it reared back before thrusting forward and pinning her to the ground.

Agony rolled through her body beyond any she had known, in this life or the last one, and she strained against the grips of those hungry mouths, the bottle still somehow in her grasp. A pulling sensation down her sides that grew worse as they began to eat, then a sickening yank and she was free.

Not all of her, she knew. If she were to look back, she would see her lower half still caught, left behind, abandoned. She didn't look because the sight might freeze her, might stop her before she could make her goal. Some of her many arms were pressed into service as legs, and she half dragged herself, half scurried until she reached the tree she was looking for, the one with the lightning struck branches. She grew weak, her lifeblood leaving her, who knew how many of her vital organs left behind.

They came after her, their appetites not sated by only half of her. They were almost on her, creatures whose bellies held parts that used to belong to her. Still, they didn't see her, not up here, and they wouldn't until it was too late. Until she'd done what she came to do. Her vision blurring, she searched the night sky.

There, a dim spot in the middle of the glowing web. Tattered where the threads had weakened, where the creatures had tried to get through. Crouching close, she gathered the frayed ends together, used her spittle to shape them for her needs. The taste was bright and crisp. Prying open the top of the bottle, she let the warmth wash over her, then reached a thin finger inside to gather the material. Working quickly, she wove it into thick, luminous strands, then joined it to the frayed ends of the damaged web.

More of the night creatures shrieked to each other, but she would finish before they could find the weakness. They wouldn't make it through, not with the strength of what she'd gathered. Trial and error it had been, when she'd first sought to protect her people from the dark. Cries of sadness, of anger, of pain, none of them were strong enough on their own to withstand the night creatures. It was only when thinking back upon her own life, her own cries, that she had realized strongest of all would be those of a mother bringing life into the world. Unfettered by social convention, not hushed by a well-meaning husband. She knew these men were only seeking to comfort their women folk, but it weakened the thread.

What she'd gathered this night glowed brighter than the threads around it, held stronger. The girl had been a fighter, and the anger had helped.

Good, thought the Midwife as she joined the final pieces together, the last work she would do in this world. She hoped it would be enough, and felt gratitude for that mother's strength, for her courage in forsaking silence. The only way to push back the night.

THE LITTLE HEAD

Elise had heard the phantom crying as long as she could remember.

A voice in the night, not her own, and not her younger sister's, as she first believed. The girls, separated in age by three years, shared a room until they were teenagers. Thinking back, Elise had a vague idea that this was when the crying had started, in those strange, hazy days between child and woman, when she started noticing everything that was wrong with herself.

It wasn't every night, and it wasn't always the same. Sometimes it seemed to come from behind her, a breathy sob over her shoulder. Other times it was in the middle of the bed, at her chest, held as close as a lover. The worst was when it was down low, at the foot of the bed. Like a monster crawling from beneath to lurk, waiting for a bare foot to present itself.

"Who's there?" she found the courage to ask, two nights after it started. The crying ceased, but there was no response. Not that night. Several nights later, when it happened again, Elise snapped her question before she could think better of it.

This time she got an answer.

"Why do you care?" A child's voice, sharp and angry.

She didn't have a response. She was too terrified, hearing the words spoken in the darkness, in what should have been an empty room.

But over time, as Elise lost sleep to the crying in the nighttime, she grew less frightened and more annoyed. A hesitant word to her mother had only elicited a purse-mouthed look, one that said Elise was far too old to be causing this kind of trouble. So, on her own, she searched the room from top to bottom, and never found a trace of whoever was crying. Not even so much as a cold spot, so she doubted the presence of a tortured spirit. Whatever the case—ghost, poltergeist, or her own fraying sanity—she decided it wasn't worth losing sleep over. Each time it awoke her, she coldly told it to suck it up. Sometimes it worked, the night going silent as the sobs were swallowed, other times it grew muffled. Still others the cries increased in pitch, and sometimes anger. That was another thing that scared her at first—after all, she'd never discovered what shared the darkness with her. What if it turned out to be dangerous? But as with many things in Elise's life, familiarity bred contempt, and she forgot to be afraid in the waves of irritation and exhaustion that accompanied the night time visits.

By the time she went off to college, she'd grown used to her roommate, as she'd begun to think of her. And it was a 'her,' no doubt about that, so at least she didn't have to feel guilty when she moved into her dorm room. She liked Karina, the girl she'd been paired with at the beginning of freshmen year. They were similar enough to enjoy one another's company without getting on each other's nerves. Over time, though, the friendship waned, then soured. Karina told Elise at the end of the spring semester she'd be looking for another roommate come fall.

"It's not you," the girl said, stuffing her oversize purple comforter into a laundry bag. "It's just that college has been an adjustment. I'm struggling some with body image, and I need to protect myself. You understand, don't you?"

Biting her lip against tears, Elise assured her that she did, but in truth she didn't understand, not really. The girls had both gained weight in the first few months of school—the dreaded freshman fifteen. But Elise had been on the lookout for exactly this kind of backsliding, and she'd orchestrated a plan to help them both get back on track. She'd thought she was helping her friend, but maybe Karina didn't want to be reminded of her failures.

That night when Elise was woken by the crying, it was the first time she didn't tell it to stop. She felt instead like crying right along with it, but she resisted the urge. For some reason it was important to her not to give in, be as weak as that phantom sob.

Over time, the cries became background noise. She found if she was firm with it, the voice would quiet itself enough for her to return to the sleep she so badly needed. When she started letting men spend the night, she'd been apprehensive, wondering if anyone else would hear those sobs and think it was her. But no one ever did. She never put it together that the voice only cried when she was alone.

Harry was the only one who ever came close. Not until after they were married, so maybe it was simply that the voice couldn't keep its sadness contained past a certain point.

One night she woke to the sobbing, and realized Harry was awake and sitting up beside her. She froze, wondering how the hell to explain it, this thing that had stalked her sleep from an early age. Because as little as she understood it, she felt responsible for the damn thing.

"Elise, baby?" came Harry's voice in the darkness. He laid a gentle hand on her hip. "What's wrong?"

She ground her teeth. He thought it was her, sobbing herself to sleep. A hatred for the voice welled up inside her, burned through her veins like poison. She had no choice but to take the fall. "Bad dream," she said finally, doing her best to sound groggy and tearful.

He laid down, spooned up behind her. "Honey, you don't have to lie to me."

She couldn't breathe, eyes wide in the darkness.

"It's gonna happen, Elise. We'll get pregnant, okay?"

She nearly bit though her own lip, pain and fury warring within her. She didn't want to talk about it. She never did, and that voice, that stupid sobbing voice, had brought it on. "It's fine," she said, and scrunched herself to the edge of the bed, feeling his warmth fall away from her.

The next morning, exhausted and staring at the blood in her panties, she screamed into the mirror.

"You bitch! You worthless, sneaking bitch," she snarled. "Three days late. For what, for fun?" Her lips curled into a snarl, and she stared at the enemy. Her body. Her stupid, betraying body.

She'd thought it would be easy. That as soon as she gave the go ahead to her eager reproductive system, she'd be knocked up. She tried not to be too upset when it didn't happen immediately, but as time wore on her resentment grew. She punished herself with exercise, with pain, with whatever she could come up with to distract herself.

"Child bearing hips, right?" she said with disgust, handfuls of soft flesh between her pinching fingers. "Cow udders?" She squeezed her heavy breasts painfully, leaving red marks in the pale flesh. "I've put up with you my whole life, and now, when you can finally be of use, you fuck me over."

She turned her back on her reflection and stepped into the shower, the bathroom fan cranked for white noise so Harry wouldn't hear her crying. Neither of them heard the bitter sobs that lasted until the water was finally turned off.

Then, so many years later that she'd given up hope, a bloom of joy and relief when Elise got the call from the fertility doctor. The treatment had worked—she was pregnant, at long last. She cried with relief, and Harry held her close, by that point far more worried about her wellbeing than he was about becoming a father. She followed all the directions, watched her calorie intake so she didn't gain too much weight or risk gestational diabetes. She got her vaccinations, took her vitamins, and kept active, even when it hurt. For eight whole months, there was peace, both in her own heart, and in her darkened bedroom each night. She nearly forgot the voice. She certainly didn't miss it.

The birth was hard, worse than she could have imagined. After nearly two full days of labor and a failed epidural, she'd finally opted for a C-section, hating her weakness the whole time. Afterward, alone for a moment in her hospital bed, she'd sobbed at the horror of it.

None of that carried over to her feelings for the baby, however. Little Patricia, with her perfect, tiny hands and feet, her sweet downy hair, and her curled up cricket legs. Elise knew every bit of what she'd gone through had been worth it. Remembering the deep depression of the days when she was trying, she knew she'd do it again in a heartbeat, if her little girl needed her.

It was two days before she could get out of bed to take a shower, and when she did, she stood before the bathroom mirror, horrified, unable to meet her own disgusted gaze. She'd expected it to be bad, but not this bad. Her legs were swollen, enormous, the shiny skin of her feet ready to split. Her face was red and tired, any trace of makeup gone, and as for her belly—Jesus. She never wanted to look at it again. She vowed to start losing weight the minute she went home, C-section be damned. She wasn't going to stay like this, not if she could help it.

But her body wasn't having it. Every time she cut calories, increased her workouts, her body clamped down, refusing to let go of its stores of fat. She sobbed over the scale, avoided the mirror, and wouldn't let Harry touch her. And to make matters worse, something was seriously awry with her lady parts.

She'd felt something bulging down there, pressing against her cervix, and was filled with dismay. Surely the one benefit of a C-section was not having to worry about a damned prolapse? She scoured the internet for ideas on how to fix it, but nothing seemed to work, and it kept getting bigger. She tried making an appointment with her OB/GYN, but it would be a month before they could see her.

"Elise," said the triage nurse in a tired voice. "A prolapse is never an emergency. It's pretty common—don't worry so much."

How could she not worry? It was a horrifying thought, her insides trying to become her outsides. She cried every time she went to the bathroom, dreading feeling the thing pressing against her, almost as if she were giving birth. And whatever anyone else said about it being painless, that wasn't the case for Elise. Her back killed her all the time and her gut was filled with wrenching spasms.

One night, sobbing from the frustration of it, Elise ran herself a hot bath and climbed in, looking away from her naked body. She grimaced as she folded herself to sit down, despising the feel of the rolls of fat that pressed against each other. She stretched out in the heat, hoping for relief, but instead a stabbing pain ran through her, followed by a rending sound that made her want to vomit. She tried to scream, but the pain was too bad, worse even than labor at the very end.

Elise clutched the sides of the tub, trying to pull herself up, to call for help, but more pain wracked her. This time it felt as though her spine were cracking, coming loose from her body, the popping sounds that accompanied the pain doing nothing to ease that fear.

"No," she managed to gasp, writhing in water now tinged pink. "What the hell is this? What's happening to me?"

The pressure at her cervix increased, her labia spreading as something pressed against them. She screamed and clawed, but she could do nothing to stop the pain.

Until a voice cut through the steamy room.

"Suck it up, Elise," it said, cold and derisive.

She was silenced, panting, listening, vaguely aware in some removed part of herself that the baby was crying, that Harry was pounding on the locked door, calling to her to let him in, but she couldn't move, couldn't even answer him.

"Who's there?" she managed.

"Why do you care?" came the voice again, and with those words, she knew. It was her nighttime roommate, returned.

"You're back," she said through gritted teeth. "Help me, please. I don't know what's happening to me." Another incredible crack of bone, and she felt her spine folding backwards, found herself looking at the back of the tub, her neck arched, her weight resting on the top of her head.

"I never left. I have always been here."

So much anger in the voice, so much hatred. Elise could hear it, but in her haze of agony she didn't care. The voice was all she had.

"Please, I'm begging you. My body—"

"I am your body, Elise. I am who you have fought with every step in this life."

"What?" she panted, before something split inside her, a shrieking, sliding heat of tearing open. She sobbed, for she had no more words, her throat constricted by the painful pressure of being arched backwards.

"You never cared for my tears. I will not care for yours."

Elise felt her skin tear open where her hip bones jutted and gargled a scream. "You're...my...body. How can you hate me so much?"

A long, sad silence, and Elise thought she might have gone deaf, the way the pain made the blood rush in her ears.

"I have asked myself that question every day for thirty-three years. I never got an answer."

She was a perfect backward arch now; her head submerged in water up to her nose, and she could see her own heels. Her spine, never meant to bend this way, snapped in three places at once with a sickening pop she felt all through her body. She couldn't expand her lungs against the press of her straining flesh, couldn't scream as her abdomen split down the middle like a zipper, her skin pulling apart, reddened muscle and yellow fat open to the air. All feeling should have been severed, the condition her spine was in but that wasn't the case. She felt everything.

"I only ever wanted to be your friend. I gave you everything you ever asked of me, no matter how unreasonable. And all I ever received in return was hatred. No more."

"If you kill me, you kill us both," she said, knowing even as she did that it was too late.

"I'm not killing either of us. I'm handing over control to someone who will love me."

There was a final, sickening pop, and her windpipe was crushed. She couldn't have spoken if she tried. Bent even further, she watched as something was birthed from her traitorous body. A head emerged, but not an infant's—a woman's, fully grown, with blood-sticky hair down to her shoulders, just like Elise.

For a moment, the two heads hung there, suspended, staring at each other. Then there was a final crack, an impossible pressure, and a feeling of being turned, somehow, inside out.

After that was darkness. When she woke hours later, she could not see or speak, and the sounds she heard were muffled. Harry's voice, filled with concern. A woman's gentle laugh, something about slipping with a razor. A voice, much like her own, but filled with love, cooing to a baby. To *her* baby, telling the girl how beautiful she was, how perfect.

Some time later, she felt the pressure of a hand from the outside, and the same voice speaking to her, with as much love as had been lavished on the infant.

"I understand, Elise," the woman said. "But I couldn't let you do it anymore. I couldn't let you do to her what you'd done to us all these years. Don't worry, I'll take care of all of us."

And since she could do no more, Elise closed her eyes, and she started to sob.

BROKEN BRANCHES

The problem with perfection is it's such a heavy load. Awkward, too—unwieldy. It's not like lifting dumbbells or bench pressing, where the weight slowly increases with your strength, and it's all condensed into an easily gripped, manageable size. It's more like being a tree, stretching your branches to fit yet one more thing. But the further out from the solid width of your trunk, the harder it is to keep steady. Each thing that comes along, each rough edged piece of your bark that needs smoothing, they're so small on their own, so how could you say no?

Part of it's your perception of yourself. Did you say something wrong, fail to supply the correct answer, the graceful response that everyone else must know by heart? Are you even sure you were wrong, or was someone just unhappy and made it your fault? Doesn't matter, the result's the same. You stretch ever further, and remember this lesson, to be still, to be careful, to be responsible for the outcome. Because those emotions that don't belong to you will swirl through your head at night, and you'll practice your answers, come up with a strategy to make it right. Usually you do, because you're good at this by now, you've had no choice but to hone these skills. But now there's one more burden down there at the very end of your branch. And you've sapped your strength not sleeping, but repairing something you never broke. Or maybe you did—accidents happen, isn't that what you tell your children? Things break, it is the nature of them, and it's imperative for them to learn not to spend so much worry on them. Yet it's not a lesson you can teach yourself, the habits of perfection and apology much too deeply ingrained in your wood. Cut you deep and see the rings of things that were never yours to own.

GODDESS of NEED

"Will you be wanting a blood sacrifice?"

The goddess's question hangs in the air, bright and coppery, the quill pen she holds hovering above the creamy page beneath.

The young goddess, newest to join the ranks of the old and revered deities, puts a hand to her chest and shakes her head. "No sacrifices," she states, careful to keep the recoil of horror from her tone.

The first goddess, Demetria, is older by millennia but timeless, her skin a burnished gold, high cheekbones sweeping up to dark, narrowed eyes. "Vegetarian, are you? Crops, then?"

Again the young goddess shakes her head and presses her lips tight. The flesh of her face is smooth and soft, the brightness of her eyes betraying her extreme youth.

A dark and damning eyebrow raises on the elder deity; the quill's feathered end brushing ancient pages with a faint, impatient swish. "How will you sustain yourself?"

The young goddess smiles. "I'll be fine."

Demetria watches her for long seconds, then makes a strike through the page. "Very well. What sort of goddess are you planning to be? What are your strengths?"

The young goddess clasps her hands before her. "I want to be a loving goddess. Nurturing, kind." She thinks for a moment, her bright eyes turning inward. "Approachable," she adds, then quivers as the ancient gaze holds hers. Demetria is most assuredly not approachable, her haughty glare and fabled temper a warning against anyone getting too close. A warrior deity, revered and feared in equal parts by her worshipers. The young goddess has never wanted to be like that.

Demetria's expression doesn't change. "Very well, but what will you be patron of? What will you do for your followers?"

The young one takes a deep breath and smiles. "Everything."

She has finally succeeded in cracking the elder spirit's stone facade. Demetria's lips purse, her brows drawing in, and the young goddess feels a change in the atmosphere. An electricity to it, and the smell of ozone—a gathering storm. She trembles, awaiting the legendary burst of anger.

It doesn't come. Instead, the quill is put to one side, and the golden eyes focus on her.

"Young one," says Demetria, her tone soft, the voice of a mother. "I have stood where you stand. I have created myself in the image I desired, of who I thought I wanted to be. I understand the wish to be everything to everyone, but it is not sustainable." She flicks her attention to the ledger and back up again. "Particularly if you will take no sustenance from your supplicants."

The young goddess shakes her head. "I want for nothing, and neither shall they. I can do this, Demetria. Believe in me."

The ancient gaze holds hers for a long, uncomfortable

moment, then the elder goddess's mouth quirks up in a smile, there and gone in the blink of an eye. In its wake, she does not look pleased.

"Your requests are noted." She moves her hand in an elegant, dismissive gesture. "Go then. They are waiting to take you." She turns her attention to the next item on her endless, celestial list, and though the young goddess quaked to feel that attention upon her, now that it is gone, she feels a sense of loss.

"One moment," calls Demetria, without looking up. "What are you calling yourself? Have you chosen a name?"

The young one shakes her head. "My people will name me, and I shall be glad of their choice."

If she is waiting for an argument, or more advice, she is disappointed. She departs the glowing presence of the eldest goddess with the uneasy sense that she has failed a test. It's a new and unwelcome feeling—the young goddess has never failed at anything. That is who she is.

Her unease slips away in the discovery of her domain, the land and people she is called to watch over. It's not large, nothing like the vast territories under Demetria's eye, but it's perfection. Lush with vegetation, humidity rises from the damp, green leaves of enormous plants. They grow outward from a wide riverbed, though the water flowing within has winnowed to a stream. That is the first thing she fixes, kneeling at the sandy bank, one hand clasped around a gnarled, protruding tree root. Plunging her hand through the burbling surface, her fingers sink into the soft silt below, touching the heart of the river that beats beneath. Closing her eyes, she opens herself, an unhindered flow of her essence and intent binding with nature, giving it strength.

A rushing noise signals her success—she steps back to watch the half-dry bed fill with water, the surface a bright silver, alive with the shadows of large fish. She claps her hands, joy sparking in her heart, and the trees around her respond. A susurration of growth whispers through the forest, leaves sprouting and unfurling from branches as they stretch their reach; thickening trunks growing taller into the cloudless, azure sky. The goddess feels the renewal in her veins, a surge of vitality filling her very being. She is connected to this place now, drawing happiness from it as she feeds the land. She pictures herself curled against the river bed, yin to its yang, two hearts beating in tandem.

It doesn't take long for the change she's wrought to bring her what she's been waiting for. There is a village down river, the life of which is tied inextricably with the water's abundance. Creeping drought in latter months has created a wearing sense of unease and doubt. Mothers worry for their children, men for their families, and herders for their sheep as the water level drops and fish grow scarce. The sudden onslaught of silvered water, sweet to the taste and full of aquatic life, brings the people to the source, hope in their hearts.

The goddess waits for her people, kneeling by the river's bank, surrounded by bounty. As the first uncertain faces appear on her horizon, her smile spreads as wide as her welcoming arms. "Come, my people," she cries, careful to soften her voice from the thunderous crack it is capable of. Fear has no place in her plan, and she is rewarded by their confidence in approaching her. Several of them kneel with her, though they keep their distance. That will change with time, she knows, once they begin to trust her.

And it does, faster than she imagined. Her people grow close to her, become familiar. They learn to bring their troubles to their goddess, and through them she learns the best ways to care for the land, to reinvigorate nature. She and the earth thrive together, and with them, the villagers under her care. The river fills its banks but never overflows; fish swim in abundance, and at harvest time, the crops reach heights and health never seen before. The people hold a special festival to honor their goddess, and to name her. Her heart overflows to see her philosophy borne out—there is no need for fear, here in her valley. All is done with love.

One day as she wanders her forest, easing nature to gentle sleep ahead of winter's bite, she feels a sudden rush of electricity, and knows she is not alone. She turns, radiant, to welcome her preceptress. Surely now Demetria will see that her trust was well-founded—the young goddess can't imagine the elder deity not being impressed with the state of her small realm. She waits in eager silence, head bowed while Demetria's gaze travels over all she has wrought. It is a long time before the warrior goddess speaks.

"What do they call you, daughter?" asks Demetria, her soft tones at odds with the stone of her expression.

The young goddess looks up, her smile shy but bright. "Ophelia. Isn't it lovely? It means helper." Her very flesh glows, giving off a faint luminescence.

"I know what it means, child."

She is gone again, no word of encouragement or praise spoken, and Ophelia is left alone, her light slightly dimmed. She shouldn't have expected anything different—Demetria is not known for effusive praise. And yet, if any situation called for it, surely what Ophelia has accomplished is worth it? She realizes she wants to see the admiration of her supplicants reflected in Demetria's eyes, and chides herself for vanity. Her people's love is enough; she needs no other.

In bleakest winter the land sleeps around Ophelia, but she is allowed no such rest. Her people's problems are, if anything, worse than ever, and they bring them in a long and endless line. Domestic squabbles, misbehaving children, jealousies and unrequited love. She knows Demetria and the other deities would not deign to listen to these kinds of troubles, but Ophelia is different. Of greatest importance is to be loving, and loved.

Soon the people build her a temple within the boundaries of their village—this way they won't have to travel so far, and can nip out to see her whenever they wish. She is gratified and touched by the gesture, but her heart sinks to leave her forest behind. Still, she is needed, and it brings her purpose and peace. They love her, which is all she ever wanted—she vows to try harder, to rise above the nagging fatigue pulling her down. It must be her absence from the land—she misses their communion, but all slumbers in winter, and she tells herself it would do her no good until spring.

Before the land thaws, she receives a visit from two neighboring goddesses, not as old as Demetria, but far more experienced than Ophelia. She is heartened by their presence, until their purpose is revealed.

"You need help," they tell her firmly. "You cannot continue as you have; you exist entirely in their realm now. That is not our way. You must set boundaries."

"You mean walls between me and my people?" she asks, voice quivering. "You may wish to treat them that way—I do not."

None of their appeals make any difference—she knows what she's doing, and she doesn't need any help. When they are gone, she turns with relief to the next in line, a woman jealous of her sister's beauty, looking for ways to feel better about herself.

"I oughtn't to trouble you with this," the woman says, hands twisting together. "Only I don't know what to do, and you're the only one who understands."

The affirmation revives Ophelia, sets her to her task with increased vigor. This is who she is: problem solver, solace, unconditional love. Helper.

When at long last winter recedes and warmth revives the land, Ophelia feels no better. If anything, she is more tired, and disheartened that spring's renewal did not rejuvenate her as it has everything else. Her exhaustion has communicated itself to the land—a man comes running into the temple, interrupting Ophelia to report with a note of hysteria that the river is drying up.

Dread fills the village, and something else. It is foreign to Ophelia, she cannot name the feeling her supplicants project at her until she remembers standing before Demetria, striving to be perfect, to not set off a storm of words. They are *annoyed* with her. Some of them are even angry, and it cuts Ophelia to the quick. She fights back tears as she hurries to her home at the mouth of the river, desperate to make things right. She tells herself goddesses do not cry, but it makes no difference to the burning behind her eyes.

More hurt awaits her at the river bed—no matter how she tries, she cannot reinvigorate the water as she once did. She puts all of herself into it, strives with all her might, but the land is as drained as she is, its resources exhausted. She stares at the thinning stream and cannot process this failure. She never fails—hard work has always been enough.

She looks out at a sea of doubtful faces, seeing more of the anger and irritation. It stings her like a swarm of bees, their disappointment a physical pain. She tries to rise but finds herself too weak.

"I am sorry," she tells her people in a small voice. "I think...I need a bit of rest." The admission is wrenched from her, she has never before needed rest, and she despises her own weakness.

The village elder kneels and takes her hand. "Of course, Ophelia," he says in a soothing voice, and his kindness only increases her tears. "You must rest, take care of yourself. That is the most important thing, to all of us."

She can only nod mutely, and he squeezes her hand before he goes, leading the rest of her people away, with one last encouraging look over his shoulder. Relief floods her as she lays next to the river, feeling the faintest pulse of its heart as she closes her eyes. All will be well, and when she awakes, her people will still love her.

Yet when next she opens her eyes, it is to the sound of shrill voices and a hand grasping her shoulder, shaking her awake. The face of the village elder looms over her, his brows up above his wrinkled face. "Ophelia? How are you feeling?"

It is several disoriented moments before she can sit up, dismayed to find herself no better. Panic in her heart drives back the fog of sleep. "How long have I slumbered?" she asks, seeking clues in the landscape, the temperature. It looks much the same. Has spring turned to fall? Why is she still so tired?

The elder lowers himself to the river bank beside her. "I hope your little rest did you good. It's been no easy task keeping everyone happy in your absence. I waited as long as I could, but you are needed, Ophelia." There is a gentle chiding in his tone that she doesn't like, but she pushes back unworthy feelings.

"Yes, of course," she says, but this time their need has no power to rejuvenate her. She is as drained as ever, the land reflecting her emptiness in dead trees and dry ground. The river itself is thinner than it has ever been, its weak flow a mirror of her own vitality.

The clamoring behind her grows louder, and she turns to find several dozen of her supplicants awaiting her, wearing expressions of irritation. Lips pursed, arms folded, and feet tapping, they crane around one another to see what the holdup is.

Despair sweeps through the young goddess and shadows gather over the sun. She tries to gird herself for the work before her, to straighten and stand, but still her legs will not hold her. She turns to the elder, tears in her eyes once more, and shakes her head. "I am sorry," she whispers. "I don't know what's wrong with me, but I cannot yet. I need more rest."

She searches his face for the kindness he showed her before, seeking not permission, but validation. Her search is in vain. His face becomes craggy with disapproval, his brows drawing together and mouth turning down. "Ophelia," he says in a tone that reminds her of her mother in unhappy ways. "We've been lenient. We've been forgiving, but enough is enough. We gave you an entire day, and now it's time to give us some answers."

Her body processes his words before her mind catches up, a dull pain throbbing in her chest, her back prickling. A day? It's only been a day? She breathes deeply and tamps down her irritation. It would do no good to quarrel, and goddesses do not argue. Instead she lifts her hands, palms open and empty. "I realize you're disappointed, but I have not my strength back yet. I need more time, more solitude to—"

He speaks over her as though she isn't there at all. "This isn't about what *you* need, it's about what *we* need. Your people—we are the ones who are weak and in pain, yet still you ignore us. You must explain yourself, convince us that you are truly too weak to work."

She tries, many times, but her words fall on deaf ears. When it becomes clear nothing will sway the man, exhaustion overwhelms her and she looks beyond him to the crowd behind. "My people," she calls weakly. "All is well, but your goddess must rest. You are a good and capable village; help one another in my absence, as you did before I came."

Nothing has prepared her for the vitriol they spew at her. Curses, accusations, even saliva flies toward her as they vent their fury. Frozen in place, she cannot respond to defend herself, to show them their error, and when they are done, as one they turn their backs on her and leave her there, empty and alone.

Ophelia has no words for the pain that courses through her veins, the burn that hollows out her stomach and wraps itself around her spine. She lies unmoving beside the dwindling river, unable even to lift her head. Her tears soak into the soil, dry and harsh beneath her cheek, but where once the land flourished alongside her, all around her retracts into fallow bitterness.

"I am a goddess," she says within the echoing confines of her own head. "How is it that I hurt? I am immortal—no blade may pierce my skin, no illness find purchase within me. I am strong enough for this. I have always been strong. Why can I not rise and try again?"

The arid landscape gives her mute answer—all things need rest, and she has allowed herself none. To rest, to retreat within herself to listen to that quiet voice means saying no. It means letting her people down, but more than that, it is the refutation of her identity. She is Ophelia, the helper. A name given, she had believed, in love, but now she wonders. It defines her only in relation to her people, to what she is to them, and leaves no room for what she had once been, or could be. In bitter silence, she realizes Demetria had been wrong. The once young goddess asked for no sacrifices from her people, but she relied on them nonetheless. It was their need that sustained her, the role she had written for herself and they gladly set the stage for. To be needed. To be wanted and valued. It was what she sought from these mortals who professed to love her, but that value was conditional. She has emptied herself, squeezed every last drop from the land she loved to fulfill their wishes and their expectations of her, but this was not altruism. It was to earn her the hollow love she thought she needed. Now she is spent, they have no further need, and withdraw from her.

Worse, they revile her. The burn in her stomach grows, her heart afire remembering the fury in their faces, the hatred. Her breath comes faster thinking of all she has given. *We gave you a day.* As though a day was all she needed to replenish and renew herself.

As though it were up to them to set such a time limit. She pushes herself up from the ground, a low wind rising and crackling dead leaves in the canopy above. More than that—as though they were being *magnanimous* by allowing her a day's grace before she resumed performing miracles at feverish speed. She seethes, teeth grinding as she uses the solid trunk of a blasted oak to get to her feet.

Heat rises in a shimmering wave around her, a wall of fury bringing small flames to life in the dead brush. It is ready kindling, the kingdom primed to burn at her feet. The remains of the river evaporate with a hiss, cracks opening in the bed beneath.

"I am a goddess," she says, this time out loud, for the first time opening her throat and reaching within to use the voice of the storm. Trees bow before her, the underbrush ablaze. "I am a goddess, and it is time they remembered."

The children notice it first; a plume of black smoke on the horizon, obscuring the forest that has been the backdrop all their lives. They tug on the hems and arms of their parents, small fingers pointing, voices rising as they seek to convey their fear. As has ever been the way, adults shush them, dismiss their fears. Nothing can happen to them—they are safe in the care of their goddess. She might have grown lazy and selfish, lying there in the river bed all day, but she would never let harm come to her people. Run along and play, and do not interrupt again.

The children return to their vigil, acrid smoke catching at the back of their throats. They cough, exchanging glances from watering eyes. Their parents are wrong. This is no ordinary smoke—can't they feel the change in the air? The wind has picked up, the black cloud growing. As it creeps toward the village, the children catch glimpses of bright red and orange. A flame, but it moves strangely, oozing in the wake of the smoke.

They look back to where their parents gather at their ease, only playing at the toil the goddess shouldered for them. The children know their words will be wasted, and they head for the highest point in the valley. A jut of stone, sister to the mountains beyond, cut off by time and distance. The grade is steep, nearly sheer in places, but the children help one another to climb, carrying the smallest of their number.

The animals follow. Dogs, cats, livestock, in ones and twos at first, until the herd breaks loose from their enclosure and heads for high ground. This catches the attention of the adults at long last, but by then, a steady cadence of thunder approaches. The villagers shade their eyes to search the horizon—thunder should be a comfort, a promise of rain to put out whatever is causing the smoke, but there's something wrong about it. It's too deliberate, too steady, and now the ground shakes with each crack.

"Something is coming!" shrieks a woman, pressing her hands to her face. She turns wild eyes to the forest, now lost to sight. "Where is Ophelia? Can she not help us?"

One of the herders, broad shouldered and middle aged, shakes his head, hands trembling. "After what was said to her? I don't think she'll be saving us." There is a tremor in his voice, and he sits down hard, looking as though he doesn't expect to get up again.

The village elder stares, mouth open. "Surely she would not abandon us in our time of need—what of the children?" He raises his voice, throwing it into the wind. "Will you not save the children, Ophelia?"

Heat swells forth from the approaching cloud, burning sweat from their brows and lips as soon as it beads. Another woman cries out, points to the mountain top where the village young have gathered, looking down upon their parents.

The herder laughs in a broken way. "The children have saved themselves."

The heat has grown worse, making their eyes ache, the hairs on their arms curl backward and crisp away. A scream cuts through the increasing murmurs of unease, and all are silenced by the sight of a man's beard burning, his flesh blackening beneath it, his rending agony the only sound. One of the women runs for water, but the troughs are empty, the water boiled away.

When his last cries choke into silence, everyone screams, running this way and that, some heading for the high ground, others back to their houses, still others to their temple, crying for their goddess. Her name on so many lips at once—surely she must hear their call.

And she does.

There are twelve of her people inside her temple when a bolt of lightning cracks it in two, the heavy roof collapsing inward to the sound of screams, until the screams cut off in grunts and gurgles.

"HERE IS YOUR GODDESS."

The voice comes from deep within the storm. It *is* the storm. Several men fall to their feet, clapping hands over their ears, but the voice vibrates within their bodies and souls. Blood pours from their ears, their mouths, their noses. One man's eyes burst in their sockets, viscous goo running down his bloody cheeks as he screams without end.

"YOU HAVE CALLED ME—ARE YOU NOT PLEASED IN MY PRESENCE?"

The roof of every dwelling bursts into flames all at once, the whoosh of the fire drawing what little air is left. Those within burn in seconds, hair crisping to nothing, skin crackling in the flames. The smell of cooking meat wafting to the mountain above makes the children groan, but the dogs and cats lick their lips.

The village square is full once more, everyone having fled their homes, the earth opening before them. Deep fissures surround the houses, cutting off all who remain, and soon an insidious red rises up to the surface. The people back away, crowding one another, their vision blurred, eyes aching. A woman is shoved too close to the creeping, crimson ooze, and screams as it burns her flesh to nothing, the bone of her ankle clearly visible until it too burns away and she falls face first into the hellish stuff.

Half mad with terror and pain, the people push away from this new threat for which they have no name, but a violent furnace blast of air drives them backward. A figure strides into their midst, twice as tall as any man, eyes burning a fiery blue from a head wreathed in flames. The terrible weight of her attention finds them, one by one, and all who look upon her fall to the ground, writhing and choking, blood and viscera crowding their mouths.

"KNOW ME AND MY POWER. KNOW WHAT I AM

CAPABLE OF, AND WHAT I WITHHELD IN MERCY."

A woman kneels before her goddess, crying tears that boil away before they reach her cheeks. "Please, goddess, Ophelia—"

Thunder cracks across the land, splitting trees in half, shifting the earth beneath.

"THAT IS NOT MY NAME."

The terrified supplicant bows her head, hands raised, breath coming in hysterical gasps that burn her lungs. "Please goddess, we know we have wronged you, we see the error of our ways. Please, give us a chance, time to make this right."

Hellfire blue eyes fixate on the woman for two beats of her doomed heart.

"I GAVE YOU A DAY."

DISTRESS CALL

The deck of the risen submarine pitched in the waves beside Sophie's vessel, silent and dark. Its name painted in blocky letters on the side—the USS *Ligeia*. A Gato Class submarine, its rounded surface low in the waves and looking every inch of its 311 foot length. Commissioned in December of 1940, it had disappeared from radar in early 1942 while carrying its full complement of sailors: six officers and fifty-four enlisted men. It was presumed sunk, all sixty souls lost, and based on the accumulation of algae coating the sides of the ship, it seemed a likely explanation for its seventy-eight year absence.

Except that didn't explain how it suddenly made it to the surface again. Sophie wasn't sure, but based on the photo and video documentation she'd seen of similarly aged wrecks, the *Ligeia* was in better shape than it should be. She damned sure wasn't going in the water to check below surface, but every part she could see was complete; rusted, but not compromised. It seemed impossible, but it appeared that even after all this time on the bottom of the ocean, the damned thing was still sea worthy.

It shouldn't be. She'd said it at least twenty times since she and her employer, Rick Atlas, had followed the distress call and found the sub. The ghost ship. Once he'd gotten a look, checked the database and discovered what they were dealing with, she'd insisted it wasn't possible. That was what she was here for, to act as Rick's voice of reason. He didn't have one himself, as he'd be the first to cheerfully admit. Your classic rich adventurer, with no perception of danger. More likable than that description implied, but still. He'd laughed at her concerns, reminded her what a find they had on their hands, and ventured into darkness through a hatch that hadn't been opened for nearly eighty years.

That had been forty minutes ago. Sophie stared through the gaping maw into the belly of the submarine, dark and empty as it had been each time she'd checked. Rick should have been back by now, no question. She hadn't been able to raise him on the radio, but he'd warned her that might be the case.

"The double hull could interfere with our signal, so don't panic if you can't get me. No need to call in the Coast Guard," he'd said.

"At what point *should* I request rescue, sir?"

He grinned and patted her cheek. "When we need it." Lowering himself from the side of his yacht, he found his footing easily on the main walking deck. "You worry too much, Soph," he called to her just before disappearing from view.

She knew she did, which was why she hadn't panicked when Rick's twenty minute timeline had passed. Or at least, she'd kept her panic on the inside and not keyed the mic to call for assistance. Instead she'd given him to thirty minutes, and then again to forty. She could see that kind of lapse, double the time he thought he'd need, especially if maneuvering below decks was complicated. Or if he'd seen something shiny, she thought irritably.

Anything beyond forty minutes though, she'd need to investigate. And it was past time for that. The sky was growing dark as thunderheads rolled in. They'd need to get back on board the *Orchid* and to a safe distance from the sub before the ocean got too heavy. "*Orchid* to Rick, please respond. *Orchid* to Rick, can you give me a fucking answer?"

Of course not. It was doubtful he'd even noticed he was out of contact, and if he had, he was probably glad to get a reprieve.

She stepped closer to the edge, leaned over as far as she dared. "Rick?" she called, trying hard to project her voice down the hatch. She received no answer.

"Fuck." She fought the feeling of dread—Rick paid her well to watch his back, in whatever scenario he created for himself. She owed it to him to suck it up and follow him. She called in her coordinates first to the nearest Coast Guard vessel as a precaution. She used to feel silly doing it, but everyone on these waters knew Rick Atlas, and none of them were surprised that he might require the occasional rescue. Mindful of her instructions, she'd omitted any mention of the sub, figuring it must be obvious to anyone who found the *Orchid* where they'd gone.

"Fine," she said to no one, and lowered herself to the deck of the *Ligeia*. "I've got this, no problem."

As she did, the radio sputtered above, and relief made her knees go wobbly. "About time, you asshole," she muttered, pulling herself back up and heading to the mic. "Rick? You forget how to read a watch?"

It wasn't Rick, but a repeat of the *Ligeia's* distress call that had led them to the wreck. *We are lost. All are lost.*

Sophie jerked away from the transmitter, shuddering at the hollow voice haunting the airways. When they first heard it, they'd tried responding, but receiving no answer, Rick assumed it was something automated. That it hadn't been able to break the surface while the ship lay at the bottom, but now it was topside again, the call had found the airways again. But why now? What triggered it? Was it on a loop of some kind? And how the hell could it possibly be transmitting after all this time? There couldn't be anyone left on board, but it made her uneasy.

After several more minutes with no answer, she dropped back to the *Ligeia*. The skies were heavy, the waves rough, and the gangway was soaked.

She held her breath as she entered the escape hatch and shined her light down the ladder that led into the main portion of the sub. She could make out nothing beneath, not even if she'd be descending into waist deep water. Surely though, Rick would have already returned if he'd been unable to penetrate far. It had to be walkable.

"So walk it," she told herself, holding the flashlight between her teeth as she descended the ladder.

The light from above disappeared faster than she could have imagined. Before her feet hit the deck below, she was enveloped in total blackness. That she could understand, but the sudden silence was eerie. The sounds of the sea above weren't just muffled, they were gone. She had the feeling of hands reaching for her from below, waiting to pull her from the ladder, and she accelerated her descent, breathless by the time she stepped off the last rung.

She shone her light throughout the tight compartment she found herself in. She expected to see walls of control panels; an obvious periscope sight. This was a cramped corridor that led to a set of bunks to her right, and impenetrable shadows to her left.

She frowned as her flashlight caught something metallic past the bunks. Moving slow, she wondered if those bunks were occupied by the remains of the missing sailors. She breathed deep of the stale air, searching for any scent of rot or decay, her skin crawling at the idea of being trapped below sea level in a tin can filled with dead bodies.

Not exactly their choice, Sophie. It wouldn't be the first time she'd found remains in her current employment, and she tried to keep her empathy intact. These sailors had families, loved ones who'd never known their fates.

Yet, when she passed the narrow bunks and found them all empty, somehow that was worse. Each one made up neatly, tight corners and flat blankets. Not even any dust or rust on the surfaces, and she frowned. Didn't stuff get dusty underwater?

She stood staring at the grouping of gold tubes that made up the far wall. No, not gold. Brass. Torpedo tubes, she realized, as polished and shiny as if they were brand new. Weird to see them up close, in person. Why had she always thought of them as cartoonish, not something belonging in the real world?

A clanging in the corridor behind brought her swinging around, her heart rate shooting up. "Rick?" she shouted. "That you?"

She'd expected the words to echo through the empty sub, but instead they were swallowed by the silence that pressed down on her. No wonder Rick hadn't heard her before—it was like being wrapped in cotton. She began to be uneasy about the air quality down here. She knew fuck-all about how submarines worked, but in any case none of the machinery was likely to be operational, so did that mean there was no clean air circulating? Had Rick suffocated, deep in the bowels of the empty ship?

She made herself stop before spinning out. The hatch was open if nothing else. Rick probably just lost track of the time and was off exploring. At least she didn't have to wonder which way to go—there was only one possibility, short of being launched out of one of those tubes.

It should have been a funny thought, but she had an image of herself wedged into one, in the dark, unable to catch her breath, and she shuddered.

"Lighten up, Sophie. This isn't *Looney Tunes*; no one's going to stuff you in a torpedo tube."

She raised the light, ready to follow it along the corridor Rick must have taken, and screamed when it illuminated a face, no more than ten feet away.

She didn't drop the flashlight, thank God, but when she swung it back to where she'd seen the face, it was gone. She stood there breathing hard, knowing it hadn't been Rick. It was a strange face, gray and blotchy, with eyes that shone silver in the flash. Was there someone else down here? Had they done something to Rick? And where the fuck had they gone?

She looked in each of the bunks, but they remained empty. She spun in a circle, stabbing each corner with the light, but found no one in its shaky glow. She stood still and listened, but still that silence pressed down upon her. She wrinkled her nose against a rotted fish odor that lingered in the still air.

Was it possible they weren't the first ones to find this vessel? Maybe there was a good explanation for why the damned thing had surfaced after all this time. An undersea salvage team? But then why hadn't they revealed themselves when Rick first climbed down?

A hollow thudding sounded from somewhere up ahead, as though someone were knocking at the hull. Sophie's imagination immediately conjured an image of a Great White stalking her in the gloomy depths; an ocean full of hungry, dead-eyed carnivores. She shook it off. Nothing short of explosives was going to breach that hull.

Two more steps and she stopped again, another sound reaching her from far away. Music. It was faint, and at first she thought she'd imagined it, the way you hear a song sometimes in the hum of traffic or the scream of a hairdryer. But no, it was definitely music. Something low, with minor chords. A recording? Still playing after all this time, in an empty ghost ship? Or Rick screwing around with his cell phone? She keyed her handheld. "Rick?" she said softly, reluctant to make too much noise. There was no answer, but the strange melody began to emit from the speaker of her radio as well. She wrestled an urge to throw the damned thing. It had to be Rick.

She needed to know, and not just to solve the mystery. There was something about the music that pulled her forward, wanting to hear it better, learn enough to make it hers.

She stepped forward, moving her light back and forth in slow arcs, trying to reach all the corners, but that wasn't possible. She was surrounded by deep shadows and stopped every few seconds when she thought she saw something out of the corner of her eye. She passed through the engine rooms, the crew's quarters with more of those neat, empty bunks, but when she stepped over the threshold into what must have been the crew's mess, her foot plunged into icy water up to her shin.

She drew back with a gasp, her grip tightening on the flashlight as she shone it at the black surface. Her breath came faster when she realized the water only got deeper. It slopped over into the crew's quarters, back the direction she'd come, and she had to clamp tight on her panic.

"Rick?" she called again, hoping like hell he'd shout back so she didn't have to wade in after him, but there was no answer. Just the music, which had grown no louder, and she didn't know how that was possible.

She looked back the way she'd come, nothing but darkness, and it gave her a jolt to realize how complete it was. She hadn't passed under any light coming from the open hatch as she'd come back by the ladder. Did that mean the storm obscured what little sun there was? Or had the hatch been shut?

"Has to be the storm," she whispered out loud, an attempt to force herself calm. She shone the light into the crew's mess once more, at the choppy surface of the water that awaited her. Why the fuck had she only donned her short wet suit? It ended well above her knees and would provide no protection from the freezing water at this depth. Were there *things* in it? The skeletal bodies of the lost crewmen? Or worse; things that still lived. Unnatural ocean creatures that haunted the deepest depths, brought up by the sub's ascension?

"You should be writing horror, dumbass, if all you're going to do is make this worse," she told herself. Rick was counting on her. She couldn't pretend anymore that everything was okay—he should have been able to hear her, and if the water level was rising, it almost certainly meant he was in trouble. She switched channels and tried the Coast Guard again, but there was nothing, just more of that music. She frowned. That couldn't be—she must be out of range, with the transmission looping back on her. She couldn't wait on rescue, so she gritted her teeth and stepped both feet into the water, her flesh freezing up to her knees.

She kicked along at a slow pace, hoping to warn off or knock away anything that might be lurking. A couple of times she squeaked when her foot made contact with something in the invisible depths, but nothing ever came back for more, so she assumed it was the usual detritus of human occupancy. She nearly made it to the next divider when something splashed behind her. Something big.

She screamed and jumped for the door, tripping over it and landing face first in the deeper water of the next compartment. She dropped the flashlight, searching frantically for it as soon as she realized what she'd done, but the murky light shone from below for only a second or two. In the momentary illumination, she found herself staring down into a face, inches below the surface. The same strange, gray complexion as the first one; the same staring, silver eyes. Then the light winked out.

Sophie spluttered and splashed, giving in fully to the panic. At first she pushed away, scrambling for distance from that awful staring face. Then logic returned. There was no one there, the image had to have been conjured by the dark and her own fear. Or, worst case, it was one of the doomed sailors, which was hardly unexpected. And face or not, she needed that fucking flashlight.

She edged forward on her hands and knees, sweeping her fingers along the grated floor. The water was up to her shoulders. She looked behind her, recalling that splash and feeling exposed as hell, but she could see nothing at all.

She forced herself to keep looking for the flashlight—it was waterproof and heavy duty, and the most likely reason it had gone off was that the switch had been pressed when it hit the bottom. "Find the flashlight, you'll be fine," she told herself, bracing for the touch of cold, dead flesh. She kept herself on task by sheer force of will.

Until her fingers passed over a thick hide of scales.

She screamed again and propelled herself backward, but there was no telling herself it wasn't what it felt like. It had moved beneath her hand and she'd felt the powerful muscles of something very big.

"Oh, Jesus," she said, her teeth chattering as she pressed

herself against a wall that bristled with dials and switches. The control room, had to be. So that meant she was close to the prow, and hopefully to Rick. She tried not to think about what it meant for him that something large and scaly was sharing the flooding ship with them.

"Rick!" she screamed. "Rick!"

Nothing, except that music. Still playing, so that had to mean Rick was okay, right? She peered into the darkness ahead, and realized there was a red glow coming from somewhere up there. It was big enough for the light to reach her back here, and just barely illuminate the black surface of the water.

There was no question of her next move. She couldn't go back, not without her flashlight and whatever had splashed into the officer's quarters behind her. Up ahead was light and music, and almost certainly her dumbass boss. Even if they were both in trouble she wouldn't be alone anymore. She just had to make her way through without being eaten by the giant fucking scaly thing. Never mind how unlikely it was that some enormous sea creature could have swum its way into the sealed submarine—the damn thing was there. She could still feel the scrape of its scales against her fingers.

The water was deep enough now that swimming was actually quicker, so she set out as fast as she could for the unlit portal to the next compartment. Officer's quarters, if she remembered the schematics correctly, and she dared to hope the water might level off when it had more places to go. When something brushed against her hip she struck out crazily, scrambling to her feet and lunging over the threshold, where thank God the water level dropped to just over her ankles. She'd been right, she thought, bracing herself against the wall beside her. The water had made its way into the quarters of the long dead officers.

Just a little farther, that was all. She ignored the swollen squelch of her shoes and didn't let herself think about what would happen if Rick was dead when she got there. She kept following the music, the deep red glow. The strange, discordant underlying layer she now recognized as the distress beacon, somehow woven in among the other notes. That made no sense, but none of this did.

In the corridor behind her, a compartment door creaked open. She wanted, so badly, to believe it was her boss, but when she turned to look, a sailor stood behind her. His face gray, blotchy, the flesh sloughing off around his mouth, his nose an empty hole. His eyes glowed a dead silver, and as she looked, Sophie saw more silver eyes glowing from each compartment door. The officers, at least, had not vanished aboard this ghost ship.

They began to move toward her, but their gaits were slow and strange. Her gaze ran down the body of the man closest to her, and she realized his uniform became something else, just below his hips. Thick, heavy scales covered what should have been his legs, which themselves had fused together. His upper body surged forward, his lower trailing, dragging a ragged tail behind him. As Sophie stared, his rotting mouth opened wide, and the music she'd been following filled the room.

For a moment, she was almost lost to it. She stared into that gaping maw, with rows upon rows of teeth, all curved inward like a python's, and she didn't move at all. The music filled her heart and calmed her, and she wondered why she could never catch the words. Then the wretched stench of the dead man's breath knocked her loose from the enchantment, and she turned and ran.

One last compartment, and this was it. The fore torpedo room, she realized, with bunks the same as in the aft room. The polished brass gleamed in the unholy red light, glowing from above each one. The water was deep again, up to her thighs, and looking down she found the surface crowded with dead, staring faces.

She didn't let herself look too closely, refused to count the carnage. What she did see, before her brain closed it off, was that many of them had limbs with gnawed edges, flesh torn and marrow sucked. Most of them wore uniforms, the same as the creatures that were slowly following her into this death trap. Still more dead men lined the walls of the room, staring and silent.

There was nowhere left to go. Sophie was stuck, here among the remains of crewmen that shouldn't be here. Men who died to appease the appetite of whatever their shipmates had become. The same creatures crowding in behind her, each with that same unnatural movement of thrust, then drag. She kept backing until she felt the press of the torpedo tube behind her. It clanged, the door having been opened at some point in the ship's unknowable lifespan. The eyes of the dead men lining the walls followed the sound, and she shuddered. She'd liked it better when she thought they couldn't move.

She glanced behind her at the tube. Would she fit in the damn thing? Claustrophobia made her chest tighten, but something big brushed against her in the standing water, and the terror that could touch her overrode that of the unknown.

She pulled herself up, thrust herself into the darkness feet first, and scrambled to close the hatch behind her. She clutched it, sightless in the pitch black, and wondered how much time she'd bought herself. Could she hold out here until the Coast Guard came to investigate? How long before they could get here, given the weather conditions? And where the hell was Rick? Was he lost amid the others, the meat torn from his bones, just another ghost to haunt the doomed submarine? Or was he in his own tube, awaiting rescue? Rescue she hadn't been able to give him. She tried her radio one more time, desperate for the sound of another human voice, but there was only that music.

Sophie waited for something to try the door from the other side, but all was silent inside the tube. Then there was a massive thrumming that spread itself throughout the ship, and she clutched harder to the door. Her stomach dipped, there was a flip of vertigo, and she realized they were diving.

"Oh, God," she moaned, thinking of the millions of gallons of black, storm-tossed ocean that now pressed down upon her. What was the dive depth of a sub this old? Did it matter? It was far too deep for her to make her way to the surface without gear—she would be cut off from any possible chance of reprieve. Panic made her breath come fast and shallow, even as her survival instinct fought to gain control. There was a way out of this for her. There had to be.

Then a new sound reached her ears. The drag and scrape of thick scales against metal, coming from the tube behind her. She went still, desperate to be wrong, but something touched her in the darkness. Before the rows of curved teeth closed on her calf, before she felt herself being pulled into a squeezing gullet and eaten alive by the ghost of something that could not be, Sophie knew that all her years of terror at the unknown denizens of the deep had been justified. There was no triumph in the discovery, and she began to scream.

VIGNETTES OF WOMANHOOD

IRON LUNG

Pacing hallways and bedrooms late at night and far from the sleep she so desperately needs. She looks from child to child, two boys whose breathing has always been fixed on her, by her. No one listens, every doctor and nurse a fight. It's her accent maybe, thick Alabama, sweet as honey. It makes them think she can be dismissed. But she won't be. Her boys, their lungs, they're her responsibility. She braces for the fight each day, listens for the catch in their chests, and will never stop worrying, or laying a hand to check for the rise and fall. The dry crunch of crackers that keep her company in the nighttime watch, and she is judged, this woman who is our sister. Whose heart and arms are wide enough for children who are not her own. Who knows that every day is a battle she is weary of fighting, but she will never goddamn stop, because they are all her babies.

STARMAN

The Starman first came for me when I was six years old. Cold, black glass hid his face from me. Strange cloth covered his body. His hands were gloved, something smooth and rubberized, but with only three fingers. He never spoke. He never made a sound at all. He only sat on a toy chest at the far end of my room, hidden in shadow that my parents could not see through.

I don't know how long he was there before I noticed him. It could have been weeks, or even months—he melded with the familiar shadows of my bedroom. One night, kept awake by bad dreams and dark thoughts, I saw the toe of his boot in a strip of moonlight that crept in through the blinds. The sight stopped my heart and I held my breath, at the age where I was still terrified of what I didn't know, but mostly expected to find relief in truth. Many times I felt that grip of fear, only to determine a moment later I was looking at a fold in a blanket, or an upside down toy. So I waited, but the boot remained a boot. Large, black and scuffed, with thick, wavy soles, coated in a fine dust that might have come from the surface of a planet

94

I didn't have a name for.

Neither of us moved as my gaze traveled up his leg, noting a jumpsuit that shone a dull white, appearing intentionally wrinkled. There were no zippers or patches, and the suit was one piece all the way up to that rounded, obsidian helmet. The face shield was obscenely large and pointed in my direction, though there was nothing behind it I could see.

My heart thudded, my breath coming shallow the way it did when I'd been crying hard. My six-year-old mind tried to come up with a rational explanation—was the suit my father's, a Halloween costume or relic of a job I'd never known he'd had? Was it a toy, or some admonitory creature like the elves that watched from hidden places at Christmas time? Was it real? Was it alive?

His chest rose, though I swore it was for the first time.

I whimpered and scooted back in my bed, knocking into the plastic headboard. I wanted to scream, to cry for my parents, but I couldn't, my throat locked and dry. We stared at each other like that until I finally fell asleep, the panic draining me past the point where fear could reach. When I woke in the morning he was gone, but there were boot prints in the carpet where he'd sat. I scuffed them with my feet without knowing why, and said nothing to my parents.

It was months before I saw him again, and somehow I'd forgotten that he'd ever been there. Maybe over time I convinced myself it had been a dream, or a hallucination. Or maybe I hadn't wanted to remember, because that would mean he could come back.

When he did, I wasn't in bed, nor was I alone in my room. It was late, well past midnight, but my mother had woken me from a sound sleep when she'd found the dirt on the steps. I'd swept it there in a fit of anger earlier in the day, resentful of endless chores and punishments. It didn't save me more than the time it would have taken to walk the dustpan to the trash can, but it was my small rebellion, an insurrection I held in my heart. I wasn't allowed to have things like that.

My mother didn't yell, she seethed. She spoke between clenched teeth and thin, colorless lips, each word an accusational thrust. I hadn't just swept dirt onto the stairs—I'd deliberately done it to make her life harder. I didn't care how hard she worked or how tired she was, how she never got a break. I was entitled, a brat, spoiled and selfish.

Tears rolled down my face, but I didn't open my mouth: there was no point in arguing. I stepped backward with each of her jabs, which angered her more, and her eyes got smaller, her body shaking with barely contained rage. I knew this wasn't really her, but I couldn't think of a way to reach her and call my real mother back. I stumbled over a toy in my path, something plastic and hard that jammed into my bare foot, and I fell backward.

I felt something strange under my hand, an object I couldn't identify. I looked down as my mother's shadow loomed over me and saw my fingers splayed along the top of a big, scuffed boot. The memory of the Starman came back all at once, and I looked up to find that empty, black glass looking down at me. Fear froze me solid for several seconds, then my mother snarled something that made me retreat further, pressed against the Starman's knee.

She hadn't seen him until that moment, and when she did, she went silent and still. I watched her face, my senses scrambling between fear of her reaction, and a desperate wish for her to become my mother again and protect me. The Starman's leg against my shoulder was solid, the fabric of his jumpsuit soft against my skin. The helmet lifted and pointed at my mother.

She said nothing, and neither did he, but her face fell

into shadow, her lips twitching into an unrecognizable shape. Not a smile, nor yet a sneer, and her eyes were wide above it. The standoff lasted for what felt like forever, until she turned and left the room, mumbling something unintelligible as she turned my light out.

Left alone in the dark with the Starman, my fear returned, and I scuttled away from him. He made no movement beyond the rise and fall of his chest, but I was afraid to get off the floor, or to do anything that might shatter the brittle silence between us. I got cold and my eyes grew heavy, and when I woke in the morning I was alone on the floor with the quilt from my bed pulled up to my chin.

Mom never mentioned the Starman. When I went downstairs the next morning, she was making toast. Not remorseful, not angry: it was as though nothing had happened. I was afraid if I brought it up, I would bring her ire back down upon me, so once again I hid the presence of my visitor. It made me wonder, though. Was he a monster from beyond our skies, or a guardian angel sent to protect me?

He slid once again from my memory, the truth of him like a black oil that wouldn't stick to the wrinkles of my child's brain. Sometimes when I saw a picture of the moon landing, or a shuttle launch, the sight of those helmeted men and women made my heart pound, my mouth dry, but childhood is filled with unnameable, barely understood terrors. It could have been the idea of all that deep, black, space, with nothing to catch you if you found yourself cut adrift. I dreamed that way, sometimes. Of an umbilicus floating before me in zero gravity, severed from what must have been home. Falling forever, arms out, nothing to ground me: a portrait of alone. It was peaceful.

Time passed. I grew taller, but not much. More confident, but not much. A shadow girl flickering around the edges of other people's lives, there one moment and gone as soon as no one was looking at me. I was never in any trouble at school. Good student, quiet, eager to please. I'd later come to view these as glaring red flags, with the benefit of adult experience and empathy, but back then, it wasn't much. People got angry. Parents got angry. It was life, and no one was beating or starving me. I was safe. I just didn't feel that way.

The next time I saw my Starman, he took my mother away. I was twelve, an awkward age, and I spent most of my time crying or trying not to. School, home, it didn't matter—I was thin-skinned, with no social skills, and received ample evidence on a daily basis that I wasn't getting anything right. All I wanted to do when I finally escaped to my upstairs bedroom was lay on my bed and listen to music. Tori Amos, Sheryl Crow, Alanis Morissette, and *The Crow* soundtrack. Music to help me sink into sadness while I contemplated whether the future held anything better for me, or if I was staring down the barrel of decades of the same. I didn't even play my music that loud, but my peace was always short lived.

Things got out of hand, like they often did, always my fault. I didn't have the right answers, the ones I should have known, and everything I said fanned the flames of my mother's smoldering temper. By then I was taller than her, by an inch or so, and my depressive eating meant I probably outweighed her, or came close. Still I cowered in her presence, that fury an unknown beast with unknowable limits. I remember wishing, maybe even praying, for her to go away and leave me alone. Just stop screaming, stop spraying my face with spittle and backing me into a corner, the way we always ended up.

I remembered that later, that I had prayed.

He stood before either of us knew he was there. Between one breath and the next he was a looming shadow at my shoulder. I looked down and saw his boot aligned with my own bare foot, felt his cold at my back, and my memory returned.

This time I didn't flinch from him. I remembered the way he'd faced the changeling of hatred that inhabited my mother from time to time, and how that empty, black glass had tamed her. Taken the fight right out of her, sent her back down the stairs to inhabit her own troubled mind, leaving me out of it. I was tired, and sick with crying, and I wanted it over. I didn't know what over meant.

I stepped aside, giving him full access to my mother, and waited for the storm to calm. The sight of him had the same silencing effect as the last time—Mom's face twisted, her mouth hung open, and the yelling stopped. She stood and panted in the middle of my bedroom, staring up at a face of onyx nothing, and my own breathing calmed. She would leave again, and I'd be okay.

But the Starman didn't stop there. He stepped closer, looked down into my mother's face, and the pace of her breathing increased. Her expression didn't change, and her eyes stayed focused where they had been, where he'd been standing seconds before. It was like she was frozen in place, and it struck me how vulnerable she was like that.

The Starman loomed closer still, leaning in, the smooth glass of his face shield almost touching my mother. I thought he might be studying her, wondering what made her tick and her springs come loose. Then he reached out and in one fluid movement, he grasped her wrist and twisted her to the floor.

She hit with barely a sound, just a muted huff of air as the breath was forced from her lungs. He must have been holding her up by her twisted wrist, supporting her body weight on that fragile joint. It would have hurt like hell but she never uttered another sound. The Starman dragged her across my carpeted bedroom floor, the fabric of his jumpsuit making a low *shooshing* sound as he moved. My mother's eyes remained fixed on the empty ceiling, her legs dragging boneless behind her.

It took me too long to react, to move away from my vantage point against the wall. The place where I'd cowered away from her, but now I didn't know where she was going, where the Starman was taking her. Muted thuds came from the narrow staircase that led to the main part of the house, and the last thing I saw was my mother's hair trailing down the steps. Curling, auburn shot with lighter threads, in need of a trim. It slinked down the last stair before the 90 degree turn took her out of sight.

I should have followed them. Maybe to stop what happened, or even just to know, to see it for myself. Instead I sat on the top step and waited for someone older than me to come and tell me what my new truth was. I didn't expect her to be gone, not forever, but that was what happened. Dad asked me questions, over and over. *What happened? Where were you?*

"Where were you?" I responded finally, and that shut him up. I didn't understand why, back then, too naive to know what his constant absences and whispered phone calls signified. I wasn't concerned with that—my parent's marriage was inherently uninteresting. I wanted to know why he'd never been there for anything else. Why he'd let me get pushed to the point where I'd offer a prayer to a dark god I didn't understand. One who was always listening, even if I couldn't see him. I couldn't ask those questions, and he wouldn't have been able to answer, anyway. Over the next weeks and months, the only question we had left centered around whether Mom was ever coming back.

Dad thought she would. He told me so every night before I went to bed, the dry skin of his face crinkling in an attempt at consolation. He was afraid of being alone with me, of having full responsibility for an adolescent, but I didn't mind it just being us. He left me alone for the most part, and life got quiet. I knew by then it would be permanent, that wherever the Starman took her, it wasn't the kind of journey that was ever round trip. I watched out my window on moonless nights, staring at the endless stars above. I didn't want her back. I was looking for him, until his memory slipped away from me again. After that I just watched the night sky and didn't understand why, only that it gave me a sense of obsidian peace.

The last time he came for me was just before I moved out to go to college, halfway across the country from a life I'd never settled into. It was late, but I couldn't sleep, staring up at the faded green glow-in-the dark stars I'd affixed to my ceiling in haphazard patterns years ago. Everybody had them back then, but mine were special. They meant more, even if the reason escaped me. I had a connection with the stars, both inside and out, and they were the only things I dreaded leaving behind.

A shadow shifted next to my bed, and when my gaze followed the movement, the Starman was there, standing between me and my lamp. As had happened every time before, all my memories of him came back at once, reflected against his blank face-plate. My breath came fast and I sat up, the covers pulled up high, but not far enough to hide him from sight.

We watched each other as the seconds ticked by, and he never moved. Fear-laced adrenaline rocketed through my veins, my stomach churning until I tasted bile at the back of my throat. "You're back," I said finally, my voice thin and dry.

He offered no response, silent as ever.

"Mom?" I asked.

The Starman gave a single shake of his head, confirming what I already knew. She wasn't coming back.

I tried to parse how I felt about it, but there was nothing much below the top layer of fear that was slowly subsiding.

"Is it my fault?" I asked, unsure if I cared what the answer was.

He gave another negatory shake, and pointed a gloved, three fingered hand behind him, where my mother had stood six years ago, and six years before that.

I didn't know if I could accept that, but I wasn't going to try tonight. I sat up straighter, letting the blanket fall to my lap. I looked at him for longer than I'd ever been allowed to, taking in his height, his slim build, his jumpsuit. It was the same one he'd worn each time he'd visited me, and that seemed right. I was the outlying planet, the far away star he came for. He needed to dress for the atmosphere, for the cold. But beneath the suit, strange knobs and ridges rose. I couldn't make sense of them, their pattern, how it would look on his uncovered skin. What was he? Where had he come from? I focused on his face shield, seeing my own expression reflected back.

"Why are you here?" I asked, wondering only after the words had escaped whether he was capable of speaking my language. He could understand it, but would his anatomy even let him form the words? I both wanted to hear his voice, and feared it.

This time he pointed at me, his hand moving slow until a single, thick finger was leveled at my chest. He left it there, unwavering, inches away from my breastbone.

"I don't understand," I said. "She's gone. I'm safe, aren't I?"

He extended the hand back again, toward the window now. To the dark sky and stars beyond.

"Out there?" I asked as my mind caught up to the full

import of what he was offering. A flash of fear returned, the feeling of endless space behind me. I dug my fingers into my bed like it was the only thing anchoring me to gravity.

The Starman brought his hands together, pulling the rubberized glove from one and extending it toward me again.

All my focus was on the small expanse of flesh I could see, the first time the Starman had laid any part of himself bare in my presence. His skin was pinkish brown, gnarled and shiny, his three digits more the shape of a crab's pincer claw, but each looked solid. They were spread wide, an open invitation. I reached out and touched him, my fingers grazing his flesh. It felt hot and mobile, as though something moved beneath the surface. His hand closed around mine, but lightly, and we both looked toward the window.

"I don't know," I said, and it was the truth. The idea of open space was terrifying, sweat breaking out on my upper lip, my hands trembling. It was too big to wrap my head around, and hostile. No guarantee I could survive out there—did the Starman have a ship? A planet to return to? I had my life planned out—college, a master's in teaching, then working in schools, keeping an eye out for children like the one I'd been. It was the first time I'd had anything to look forward to since the magic of Christmas died years ago. It was a future I wanted, could envision. Out there among the cold stars was a complete unknown.

So why did the idea of letting go of the Starman's hand fill me with such melancholy? I could see myself walking to the window with him, stepping out into the night like Wendy with Peter Pan, flying through the dark in the clothes I slept in. I'd never sought exhilaration, wasn't even sure I'd ever felt it. I was a fearful, mousy soul, afraid of losing my way, of never coming back.

And that was a certainty. The Starman only offered one-way journeys. Mom never came back, and I didn't believe she was flying through the cosmos. She was dead and gone, by methods unknown. It was possible she'd suffered. If I went with him, the Starman might kill me, too. I didn't think so—he'd given my mother no choice. There'd been no hand extended, just a swift departure, her head banging every step on her way out of my life. I didn't believe he would do that to me, but I didn't know.

"I want to," I whispered. "But I can't."

He watched me from behind his helmet for several seconds more before he dropped my hand and fitted his glove back on. Was he disappointed? Angry? Sad?

Would I ever get another chance?

I was too slow to find my voice, and he was gone before I could ask. My bedroom seemed emptier than it had before he'd appeared, and a deep loneliness took hold of my insides. It felt like part of me had gone with him, my future splitting into two selves, one of whom was getting further away by the second. I threw my covers back and went to the window, wondering if I could catch a glimpse of him. I didn't, but I sat up for a long time watching, determined this time to hold tight to my memories of him.

But of course I didn't. I had no control over that, and though I wrote some of it down, the ink on those pages faded and ran, and later when I flipped through my notebook, I tore them out and threw them away. They were useless after all, illegible, so whatever thoughts I'd scribbled there were lost.

Years passed. I finished college, stayed on track and became a middle school science teacher, focusing on studying outer space, my classroom walls papered with pictures of the surface of the moon, the vastness of the stars. In my head was where I kept the other facts I'd gathered, the images I'd seen of everything that can kill you in space. It was a macabre obsession, poring over stories of space flight disasters: explosions, decompression, solar flares. I was equal parts drawn to that great, dark unknown, and terrified by the inhospitable environment. Humans are survivors, it's coded in our DNA, but in space, help is either non-existent or too far away to matter.

I didn't lay that on the kids, though. I wanted them to be excited, to focus on the possibilities and all the things we didn't know. I'd chosen middle school because it was the most vulnerable age group, the most in need of help, and the least likely to ask for it. It didn't come easy: I battled against bureaucracy everyday, an avalanche of it, determined to get in the way of me making a difference. And the kids weren't always open to help, even the ones who were in real trouble. I hadn't counted on how inured they were to their lives, but I should have. Mine had seemed normal to me, way back when. Still I pushed on, growing tired but never disillusioned. There were nights, though, when I sat at my bedroom window and watched the skies. I felt like I'd lost something out there, someone I could have been, and I wondered if it was her I was looking for.

The Starman never came for me again, after that last time, his offer of a life path that branched far from my own. The next time I saw him, he was there for my daughter.

I hadn't planned on becoming a mother. I was afraid I couldn't do it right, that some hidden darkness inside me would spring free, turning me into a fury-spewing version of myself. By the time I got pregnant with Madeline, those fears had faded in the face of my work with children. I was patient with my students, thoughtful, and careful of their emotions. I thought I was safe; that she was safe. I dropped my guard against the worst parts of myself.

Madeline's father worked third shift, something I didn't

foresee as being a problem before she was born. But those were long nights with no sleep, and long days with even less. I was alone with my baby most of the time, and though I loved her with my entire soul, I felt my patience fraying. One night when she was six weeks old, she'd been crying non-stop, resisting all my efforts to get her to sleep. I thought I'd finally done it, as her heavy lids had slowly closed, her dimpled chin falling to her chest. I held my breath, counted to twenty. When she didn't move, I eased from the floor by her crib. Her eyes popped open and she began to shriek, as far from rest as she'd ever been.

I felt exhaustion in every cell of my body, pressing down on me with a physical weight. I burst into tears myself. "Fine," I snarled, lurching to my feet. "Take care of your damn self."

Her cries escalated as I stumbled to her bedroom door, guilt already gnawing at my heart, but I had to get out. I had to breathe without the pressure of constant demands for my attention, so I kept going, though she was swiftly working herself into a purple fit.

I closed the door behind me, and the noise was gone. Like flipping a switch, and for a moment I wondered if that was what she'd needed—solitude, perhaps, or one more good fuss to send her to dreamland. I wanted to feel relief, to take the break I'd sought, but the silence was so wrong. A cold dread settled into my belly. With shaking hands, I opened the nursery door again and went to her crib.

Madeline was quiet, her blue eyes open wide, but her feet were kicking, her lips blowing little spit bubbles. The looming fear of SIDS settled back into my hind brain, and I stood and watched her. Her fuzzy gaze pointed straight up, beyond where the useless mobile spun in lazy circles. My eyes followed her sight line, where they caught on a light hanging midway up the wall. There was no light there—the wall behind my daughter's crib was painted with a mural of stars in a purple sky.

My heart froze, two beats ahead of my brain. I was seeing Madeline's unicorn night light on the opposite wall, reflected on a smooth, glass surface. My breath coming quick and shallow, my hands like blocks of ice, I searched the darkness for what I knew I'd see. The Starman resolved from the shadows, needing only my notice to reveal himself, looming over my baby, close enough to touch her. He was still and silent while my memories slid back in place, those missing pieces restored. A stab of regret for the choice I'd made all those years ago—a life among the stars, silent peace and dark flight. Myself reflected in his blank face shield, the me I could have been staring back at me, distorted.

But that wasn't why he was here. Not this time. His empty gaze was on me, his very presence an admonition. I was fucking up. Becoming my mother, as I'd vowed never to do. Everything came back in full force. Every aching memory of a hurt left unaddressed, an explosive reaction to an innocent omission, the knowledge that at any time the earth could tilt beneath my feet and deposit me in some half world, where people looked like themselves but behaved like dangerous strangers.

Tears streaked my cheeks, shame at my short temper making me feel like the worst kind of mother. I looked at my little girl, her sweet rounded cheeks, her chubby hands with perfect tiny knuckles, and felt the weight of my failures. Any ache for the life not chosen was swept away—had I gone with the Starman when he'd asked, I would never have had Madeline. Nothing could make up for that, and the thought of that regret twisted my heart.

I looked back into the unforgiving, blank visage of the Starman. "Are you here to take me, then? Like you did my mother?"

He said nothing, and his hands remained at his sides. I thought of when he'd reached for me, the three strange digits offering to take me to the stars. I knew the next time he reached for me, I'd have no choice, and it would be my head bumping down the stairs on the way out of my daughter's life.

I slid to the floor where I could be close to Madeline and watched her eyes close, her chest rise and fall. She slept, but I did not.

Not then, and very little in the following days. I had to stay vigilant against myself, and the Starman. This time my memories didn't fade, and instead I saw him in every dark corner of the house, no matter the time of day. He wasn't really there, just his specter, reminding me. Warning me to walk the line lest I be flung to the heavens.

Fatigue drained me, but fear kept me going. That little spike of adrenaline that shot through my body each time I imagined those unforgiving boots, or a reflection in a place where there shouldn't be one. When I was too tired to move, I sat with Madeline and watched her with hungry eyes. As hard as I was trying, as much as I suppressed my impatience, it felt as though our time together was short. All my old fears bubbled to the surface, until I could barely move for fear of something happening to my baby. My mind ran a constant loop of images from hell—the worst possible occurrence in every situation. If I shaved my legs, I pictured the razor slicing my sweet girl's skin. If I turned on a gas burner, I saw the flame burning her flesh. Each time I filled up the tub for her bath, I checked the water temperature over and over, terrified of scalding her. The pictures in my head wouldn't stop coming, and they filled me with horror. There was no desire to carry out any of these terrors, but what kind of mother was I, that they came to mind at all?

My husband noticed, and so did my few friends. They told me to give myself grace, that no one had to get it perfect all the time. They didn't understand. They didn't know the dark depths I guarded against.

It made no difference. No matter how strictly I policed myself, no matter how hard I prayed for patience, I could feel my temper rising, becoming a beast I wouldn't be able to control for long. I don't know when I reached the decision to go, coming upon it gradually, but once I acknowledged it, the Starman was there.

I'd been expecting him, and looked at him from streaming eyes. "Give me a moment?" I asked.

He didn't answer, but neither did he stop me when I made my way to Madeline's crib. She slept in a yellow, footed pajama onesie, her small hands curled into fists up by her head. I didn't want to wake her, so I just looked, and grief threatened to engulf me. My chest was tight, my heart breaking at the knowledge of what I was giving up. I'd never see my girl take her first steps, or start school, or find her own path apart from her parents and her past.

But neither would I burden her. She could step onto whatever path she chose without anything weighing her down. And if I were honest, there was relief in the decision to let go. I wasn't good enough, never would be, and it was freeing to give up trying. I could finally become that other self, choosing one loss over another. The Starman stood at my shoulder, and I took a step back from my daughter, ready to give myself to his care.

I stepped onto nothing, my foot plunging into a void, my weight already off balance, and down I went, backward into blackness. My stomach flipped and fear froze my lungs, but even I couldn't hear my scream as I drifted downward. A slow flight away from everything I knew, my tether to the world severed and getting further away. I could still see my daughter, growing smaller as I fell. It was the peace I'd dreamed of, but the fear as well. I was weightless and so damn cold, ice crystals forming at the corners of my eyes. I struggled to take another breath and found that it wasn't fear that had locked my chest: there was no air in space. Panic hit me and I looked for the Starman—this wasn't right. He was down below me looking up, one hand on the rail of Madeline's crib.

Why? I tried to scream the question but I had no voice and no air. My lungs had collapsed and I felt them freezing, my organs being crushed in slow motion. My vision blurred as the pressure squeezed my eyes but I could still make out his hand coming up to his helmet, the face plate rising. Obsidian nothing was replaced with a visage that sliced through what remained of my sanity.

It was my own face, ravaged from years of radiation exposure, the burn of solar flares, the collision of subatomic particles. The version of me that stared back at myself had no nose, the hole where it should have been covered over by twisted, melted flesh. One eye had slid halfway down the cheek, and teeth were exposed in the thin parts of the flesh of its jowls. Still I recognized myself, and the other side of regret. She—I—had made another choice, and now she wanted what I had instead of what she'd become. The last thing I saw before the oxygen-drained blood hit my brain was a hand of melded digits reaching into the crib for my little girl. And I'd been right—the release of consciousness and life came as a relief from the agony of feeling my body freeze and crush from the inside out. I became one with the dead space beyond our world, endlessly adrift in the dark.

ONE OF THOSE FACES

Today I am Sandy. I smooth the sleeves of the too-tight sweater she brought me, purse my lips at the way her jeans pinch at my hips, the uncomfortable spill of muffin top. I'm not shaped like her at all, and the effect of wearing her clothes is incongruous and lumpy. He won't see that—I don't know why, but they never do. Maybe all they notice is my face, or maybe the impression all blends together and they see what they want to. I look in the mirror and see only myself, which is what *I* want to see. Just me, in my own clothes that fit my body and personality, but Sandy's already transferred the first payment to my account, and I don't want to have to refund it. So for today, I'll be her, take care of her problem and we can go our separate ways.

I pull up the Notes app on my phone, open the one with her name. There's a list of attributes, points of interest, and observations I made about how she moves and talks. I roll my neck, shake my hands out and practice: the way her left shoulder is always higher than her right, a flinch that never ends. The way she chews her bottom lip until it's bloody, and how she blinks too long when she gets anxious. I work at it until I get her quirks in sync, then I consult the schedule she gave me. French class ends at 10:45AM, then a quick walk to grab a black coffee at the student cafe in the library. That's where he'll be, looking for her like he does every day. She's tried hiding, changing her routine, even transferring classes, but he always finds her.

Today, he'll find me.

I draw little notice when I reach campus, take the long walk from the big parking lot instead of waiting for the bus. Same as I did when I was a student here. Old habits die hard, and I didn't think to ask for Sandy's routine in that aspect, but I doubt it matters. If all the other differences don't make it obvious that we're not interchangeable, nothing will.

Every so often a woman meets my eye, gives the slightest nod and moves past without stopping. I don't acknowledge them, but I notice. I've been here a number of times since I figured out my particular calling—college campuses are ripe for the work I do. I don't know if it's good or bad that I get recognized now—the point in what I do is anonymity, and I don't know if being seen as myself too often will break the spell, but there's nothing I can do about it. I've been blending into the scenery my whole life, and it's disconcerting when gazes stop on me instead of sliding past. Years ago, as a teenager, I'd have given anything to be noticed. But I'll age out of places like this before long and it won't matter anyway. For now it works: the signs of aging fade into the background when I'm face to face with whoever's doing the wanting.

I stop and check the time on my phone. I'm perpetually early, a side effect of anxiety, but it's better than being late. I kill time by reading the notice boards, calls for roommates and study partners and, in one instance, a weekly meet-up for an esoteric spiritual study group. "Come as you are," the flier states. Most of the flapping little slips of paper with the organizer's email are gone, and I wonder what would happen if I showed up at a place like that. Would anyone see me, if I came as myself?

"Sandy?"

The voice comes from behind me and I jerk my head up, adrenaline hitting my bloodstream hard. I'd let myself drift and I'm not prepared, but the speaker is a young woman with a short blonde ponytail. She frowns when I turn and face her.

"Oh, sorry," she says. "I thought I recognized that sweater. And the way you were standing, with your shoulder up—I thought you were my friend."

It's jarring to realize I was still imitating Sandy's tics without knowing it. Good in some ways, because I haven't blown this job, but I wonder when my subconscious started doing that. Have I been sinking that far into my role every time? Do I keep doing it after I'm finished, holding onto someone else's personality in lieu of my own? Am I anyone at all in the in-between times?

I bite my lower lip and smile, aware of how awkward it looks. I'm not sure why I do it, since this girl isn't who I need to convince. I realize with a rush of irritation it's because of the last thing she said—*I thought you were my friend.*

How many times had I said that in my life, or thought it once I learned how pathetic it sounded out loud. *I thought you were my friend...*until whoever it was proved without a doubt that they weren't. Nervous and eager to please, but without the ability to read a room and make myself seem human, I was a prime target for it all my life. Until I stopped trying, rejected any offers of friendship since I couldn't trust they were real. It was safer that way, but lonely, too, and her words open a hole in my gut.

The girl's about to leave because I can't think of anything

to say to make her stay, but she stops, cocks her head and studies me. "It's so weird. You don't look like her, not really, but you remind me of her."

"I've just got one of those faces," I say. Another phrase that trips too easily off my tongue.

She shakes her head and her ponytail bobs. "It's not that, it's more the things you do—she bites her lip like that, and the way you blink…"

I fight the urge to keep doing those things so she'll stay and talk to me. It's getting close to show time, and I need to get to the cafe.

I try to shrug like myself, but I can't remember how. What are my tics? My quirks? What are the things I do that would make someone see a stranger across the quad and recognize them as me? My mind is blank and I feel panicky. I can't stop being Sandy if I can't remember who I am, but I don't have time for an existential crisis.

"Sorry, not her," I say, wondering who I sound like when I speak. I leave the girl behind and hurry to the library, checking my phone again as I go. Shit, I'm late. If I miss him here, I might have to go through this whole thing again tomorrow, and Sandy won't like that. She's a conscientious student, didn't want to miss class today and certainly won't want to again tomorrow. I move faster, wincing at the feel of sweat trickling down my back. I never noticed Sandy sweating.

I'm in line at the cafe, holding a strap of Sandy's backpack with one hand, looking up at the menu when a shadow falls over me and a voice is in my ear.

"Hello, beautiful," he murmurs, close enough to make my hair move and my ear itch.

I startle, my left shoulder going up even higher, my lower lip caught in my teeth. I taste blood and turn to face him, today's target: Brock Kirkland.

He's tall, a bit gangly, his upper back and neck bent in a constant stoop. Not unattractive, and I wonder what's made him lock onto this kind of stalking behavior. But I know better than most that looks don't always matter.

There's a stab of apprehension in my chest, waiting for his gaze to travel over me, wondering what he'll see. Every time it's the same, but it doesn't stop me questioning if this will be where it comes to an end.

But there's no flicker of doubt in his dark eyes. He reaches out to move my hair behind my shoulder. "You're late today—I was getting worried." His words are disconcerting—I can feel the anger radiating from him, hear it in the bite of his voice, but he won't acknowledge it. If he doesn't own his anger outright, then my reaction to it would be overblown, melodramatic.

I give a nervous smile, and the split I've opened in my bottom lip widens. More blood blooms there until I lick it away.

The guy's own smile creeps further up his flushed cheeks. Is it because he saw my tongue, or because I tried to smile? Either act could be an invitation.

This is where Sandy would turn away, give him her back and hope he'd get the hint. She's given him plenty of hints, in the months this guy's been trailing her, but he's deaf to any answer but yes. If this were a real undercover operation, the kind where I needed to stay true to my role, I'd turn away, too. But my job is both easier and harder than that. I've never met Brock, but I already know him. He won't be suspicious when I give in, because he's been expecting it forever. Put enough effort and time into a woman and she'll eventually sleep with you. It's the only equation he knows.

He stays close while the line moves slowly, neither of us speaking. He looms over my shoulder, his presence making my flesh prickle, his attention like a deep itch. Finally it's my turn and I order my coffee. Brock orders nothing, ignoring the young man behind the register like he doesn't exist. Maybe he doesn't, any more than I do when I'm not playing a role. We're both transient spirits, visible only as background characters lending support to the stars of the show.

When I retrieve my cup from the end of the counter, Brock's right there, his fury crackling beneath every move he makes. It's scary, being the focus of his attention, but at least I know which way this one will go.

"Listen, Sandy, this is getting old, isn't it? I think I've done enough to prove myself." Again, the rage is just under the surface, rippling beneath his expression like a parasite. This will be over quick.

"We can't talk here," I say, looking around at the crowd of between-class students. The last thing I want is to leave the protective presence of other people, but I want to get to the point. I don't get paid by the hour.

His chin lifts. "Why not? What's wrong with here? It's our special place, where we always meet up."

Meet up. Like Sandy has any say in it. I think again of the meet-up group from the flier, picturing women with their own fluttering tabs. Inert and waiting while fingers fumble over the invitation of their presence, pulling pieces off one by one.

"I'd rather talk in private," I say, not meeting his eyes, both hands clutched around my coffee cup. I want to throw it at him, but I won't.

The smile that sweeps across his face is all teeth and he takes my arm, guiding me roughly through the library until we're outside, behind the far side of the building. There's a dumpster there, awaiting the cleanup of a repair project, and he pulls us out of sight.

I set my coffee on the edge of a stone planter. I don't want to get burned. Before Brock can say anything I straighten and look him in the eye. "I've tried telling you every way I know how. I don't like you, I don't want to spend time with you, and I wouldn't fuck you if you were the last man on earth."

The words are Sandy's, spilled out with anguish and her own fury. I like to use the clients' own phrases, ask them what they'd say to the target if there were no consequences. Sometimes it takes a while to coax it out of them, but most of the time they spit it out with white hot speed. The words they've been desperate to say but haven't because of what will happen next.

I brace myself but not much. I've learned over time that tension makes for sore muscles, so I slacken my stance as much as I can. Brock's eyes harden, his face flames and his hands transfer from the straps of his backpack to my body.

"You fucking *slut*," he snarls, and goes straight for my shoulders, knocking me to the ground.

I could have saved myself, locked my legs and ridden his weak attempt, but it's easier this way. I catch the fall on my ass where it'll heal faster. I stay down. This is the hardest part; waiting for him to finish. He looms over me, teeth bared, spittle flying from his chapped lips as he calls me every name he can think of. Cunt, whore, bitch, they all come flying at me but bounce off my armor like Teflon. I've heard them so many times they've lost meaning.

He's wearing himself out with words, and I let myself hope this is where it'll end, but then he kneels over me, his body pressed to mine. I'm afraid I've miscalculated, that this is going a whole other direction, and my stomach tightens, fear making me cold. He lands a blow to my belly and slaps my face almost in one move, and while I roll to my side and clutch my gut, he pulls himself off and wipes his mouth on his sleeve.

"You could have made this so easy, Sandy," he growls. "Now you'll never know how good it could have been with me. I wouldn't touch your skanky ass with someone else's dick." He takes off, his steps fast and jerky, looking around for witnesses as he goes.

I lay curled on my side for another minute or so, letting the deep ache in my stomach ease, relief flooding my body. It's over. Once I can stand I push to my feet and brush myself off. Someone asks if I'm okay and I nod without looking at them. I head to my car as fast as I can, keeping an eye out for Brock as I go. There's no point in relaxing my guard—they've been known to come back looking for seconds.

Sandy's waiting for me in the parking lot and I frown when I see her.

"I told you I'd call you when it was done."

She looks me over, chewing that lower lip into ground beef. "I was worried. I know you said you wouldn't get hurt, but look at you. What did he do?"

Her blue eyes fill with tears and I don't know whether they're for me, or the fear of knowing that's what her target had in store for her.

I straighten and hand her backpack to her. "Nothing I haven't handled before. It wasn't bad, really."

She doesn't believe me, wants to linger after paying me the second half of what she owes, but I'm telling the truth. It's not fun, being someone's punching bag, but the hurts, they aren't meant for me. I'm just a stand in, always have been, and the pain doesn't last long. I have a skill, one I've managed to monetize. I can be any woman, any bullseye for the kind of attention no one wants. I know how to ride a punch, how to minimize the damage to my body, and once the transaction's over, everyone's better. Brock will leave her alone now, having proved his point, and he'll find someone else to focus on. Sandy can go back to her life, until she becomes someone else's target. There's an unfortunate amount of repeat business in my profession, but at least it's job security.

Sandy hugs me before she goes; thanks me in a fervent voice. She can't quite believe it's over—that part will take a few days to sink in, but I feel a flicker of satisfaction at a job well done. I sit in my car after, looking my face over in the vanity mirror. My cheek is red where he slapped me, and there's a small abrasion where my chin scraped the asphalt, but nothing that won't heal.

I stare for a little while longer, studying my features, trying to remember which are mine, and which are hers. Maybe it doesn't matter—in the end we're all interchangeable. One will do just as well as another, haven't I proved that time and again?

I start my car and catch my own eye in the rear view.

Today I am Sandy. Next week I'll be Angela, a woman I don't know yet but will soon. I remember every woman I've ever been. Someone has to keep track. Someone has to know where one of us ends, and the others begin.

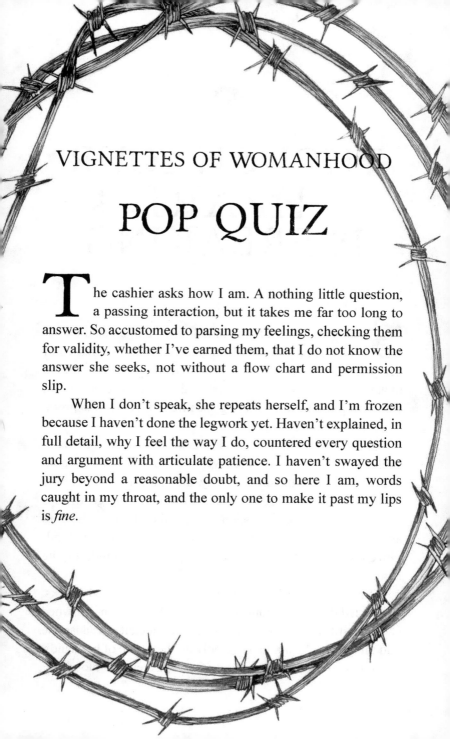

VIGNETTES OF WOMANHOOD

POP QUIZ

The cashier asks how I am. A nothing little question, a passing interaction, but it takes me far too long to answer. So accustomed to parsing my feelings, checking them for validity, whether I've earned them, that I do not know the answer she seeks, not without a flow chart and permission slip.

When I don't speak, she repeats herself, and I'm frozen because I haven't done the legwork yet. Haven't explained, in full detail, why I feel the way I do, countered every question and argument with articulate patience. I haven't swayed the jury beyond a reasonable doubt, and so here I am, words caught in my throat, and the only one to make it past my lips is *fine*.

THOUGH YOUR
HEART
IS BREAKING

Sarah stared down at the blood, dried and crusted on her hands. It had woven itself into the smallest creases of her palms, and she had a memory, fleeting, of how they'd looked when the blood was fresh. Like shiny leather gloves, elbow length. The kind of thing she might have worn to prom, back when she'd been young.

Now the blood had faded, cracked and rusty brown. It peeled and flaked away whenever she moved, and she could tell it was driving the officer crazy, the one who was standing in the corner, watching her. Babysitting until the grown-ups returned, with more questions Sarah didn't know how to answer. The strongest images in her mind were of her blood-gloved hands, and snatches of a song, one she couldn't quite name.

She turned her hands over and stared at the teeth marks, embedded deep in all four fingers of each hand. She frowned at them, still trying to discern what they meant. Because the odd thing was, the marks were only on the inside of her hands. Nothing marred the flesh of the outside, except the blood.

Helena stared at the body, one hand cupping her elbow, her free palm across her mouth. Dark eyebrows bunched; lips tight. Thinking.

"That is, hands down, the grossest thing I've ever seen."

She glanced at Max, but he didn't look like he was going to toss his cookies. He bent close to the dead man's neck, trying to get a visual on the inside of the throat, thinking there might be something in there, *Silence of the Lambs* style. It wasn't a bad idea, and Helena marked another point in the invisible score book she kept for all new partners.

"It reminds me of something," she said, walking another slow circle around the kitchen chair where the dead man slumped.

Max straightened, shook his head. "No way. Nothing like this has *ever* come across. I'd know. I'd remember something like that."

Max was young, early thirties, and the newest detective on Helena's squad, but he'd spent years studying and organizing the evidence archives, seeing all the cases that came through over the years and searching out the cold ones, looking for patterns everyone else had missed.

She shook her head. "I don't think it was a case... something else. I can't quite..."

Taylor Eckles snapped another photo, standing on a step stool and aiming down into the exposed airway. "Looks almost like a weird kinda fuckin' muppet, the way his face is spread like that."

Max shot her a look, but Helena snapped her fingers.

"*Beetlejuice*. That's what it reminds me of."

Max moved to her shoulder, craned his head. "That old movie with the crazy Baldwin dude? I don't see it."

"It was one of the scenes after they cross to the other side, when they're trying to scare the family. Geena Davis's head's all stretched out, her eyes are in her mouth? That's kinda what this looks like."

Max frowned, fished his phone out and a short search later, gave her a hesitant hand waggle. "I guess so. The way the teeth are, maybe."

The victim, thirty-seven-year-old Kevin Tudor, had his upper and lower jaw broken. They'd been snapped back so far, it was like someone had crammed their hands down his throat and pulled in opposite directions. The result was a head broken nearly in half, starting at the guy's mouth. The halves lay open, teeth exposed on either side, giving a direct view down the guy's gullet. Torn skin hung in flaps where his cheeks had once been. Helena thought she could even make out the flaccid remains of a dimple, before deciding she should probably stop looking.

"Ready to head back?" asked Max when she turned her back on the corpse. There was more than a little relief in his voice.

She sighed. "I guess. I still don't think it was her."

He scrunched his mouth to one side. "You just don't want it to be her."

"C'mon, Maxie, you see that little thing having the upper body strength to rip that guy's face in half?"

He shrugged. "Maybe she used something, an instrument of some kind. She could've—"

Helena scowled. "Who the fuck is humming that song? It's driving me crazy."

Max raised an eyebrow. "I don't hear anything. What song is it?"

She listened, but it was gone. "Fuck if I know. Something old, I think." She raised a finger. "Refrain from making the obvious jokes, please."

Max sniffed. "I *never* make obvious jokes. Can we go back now?"

Helena tossed her gloves and booties into the waiting evidence bag. "Yeah. I've got more questions."

Helena grabbed a bottled water and a couple pieces of dark chocolate from the stash at her desk. She tapped on the door and Randy Bellows, the cop she'd put on babysitting duty, squeezed past her on his way out the door. She glowered and stood her ground.

"Sorry, ma'am. Close quarters." He grinned down at her, and she crossed her arms, shoved into his space.

"I don't give a fuck how close the quarters are. You brush my tits like that again, you're gonna lose a hand."

"Sorry, ma'am." He wasn't, and didn't care if she knew it. He would before too long.

Bellows leaned against the wall instead of fucking off like he should have. "That's an odd bird in there."

She didn't ask him to elaborate. Usually she appreciated observations from her team, but Randy Bellows wasn't on her team, he just wanted to be.

He didn't take the hint, looking over his shoulder through the one-way glass. "I still can't picture how she overpowered him, a big guy like that." He waited, but when she didn't answer, he finally pushed off the wall. "Anyway, hope you got some more insight on your little field trip, and didn't just go for Chinese." He smirked, clapped Max on the shoulder and kept walking.

Max watching dispassionately. "I'm sure he thinks that's hilarious."

"I'm sure he does."

"Do you think he knows I'm Korean and he's trying to be a prick, or does he actually think all Asians come from China?"

"I'm not in his head, Max. Thank Christ. You coming?"

He shuffled into the room behind her, and Helena sat across from the blood covered woman. She opened the bottle of water and pushed it across the table, then followed it up with the chocolate.

Sarah stared down at the foil wrapped pieces and smiled. "Thank you."

"You're welcome. You want to wash your hands first?" The evidence techs had already processed the woman, taken samples from under her nails and photographed everything. Helena didn't understand why they hadn't cleaned her up after.

The other woman shook her head. "I don't think so. I'm trying to...remember." She held her hands out in front of her, frowning at them.

Helena sat back, avoided Max's eyes. "You don't remember what happened?"

"Not...exactly, no. I saw the body, though. I know what it looks like." She raised her hands. "What this looks like."

Helena nodded. "So, you understand why you're here, then."

Sarah smiled again, a small amount of color returning to her pallid face. "I do."

"So why don't you start with how you knew the victim?"

She frowned; eyebrows drawn down. "I don't know who—oh. You mean him."

"Right. Kevin Tudor. How'd you know him?"

Sarah shook her head. "Oh, I didn't. Not at all."

Helena frowned. "Then how did he come to be in your

home?"

The woman's eyes slid to the side; her lips parted. "I... well, I believe I asked him in."

Helena's eyes flicked to Max's face, but he was frowning, concentrating on Sarah. No smirk or judgment. Good. Give the kid another star.

"And did you ask him in for...romantic purposes?"

Sarah laughed. "Sex, you mean? No, I didn't, but it may have been what he thought."

Helena leaned forward. "Was he coming on to you? A sexual assault?"

Max coughed—leading, she knew she was doing it. But she wanted to understand. And yeah, she wanted the circumstances to be mitigating. There was something calm and a little broken about the woman sitting in front of her. But there was also something strong and shining that Helena felt herself responding to.

The other woman shook her head, looked into her lap. "It wasn't like that."

Helena had never been good at waiting, but she tried, giving the suspect space. Finally, Sarah lifted her head.

"Do you remember, Detective, the absolute worst time someone told you to smile?"

Helena's breath caught in her chest. She did, with vivid clarity. She didn't need to look at Max to know he was confused; it wasn't a thing men dealt with.

The woman was waiting for a response.

"I do," she said, and left it at that. It wasn't a memory she wanted to recount. Standing in line at a Dollar General, a pack of maxi pads in one hand. Feeling the hope sliding down her leg, for the baby she'd wanted for so long. Nine days late she'd been, after three years of trying. It wasn't enough. She'd barely held herself together, then she heard the man behind her in line, in a loud whisper to his girlfriend.

"Would it kill her to smile? Jesus, like I want to look at a face like that."

If she hadn't been so hollow inside, Helena might have socked him. Punched him in the dick and asked him why he wasn't smiling through the pain. But the hurt of the other was too near, too heavy, so she just paid for her pads and went home to cry.

She didn't say any of that here, now, because the grief of that time in her life was still too close, even a decade later. There'd never been a baby, and now there never would be. But even though she didn't say it, she felt like Sarah read it on her. The other woman reached out with her blood covered hand before stopping herself.

"I can see you do. I can, too. A lot of us do. You want to hear mine?"

Helena nodded.

Sarah turned to watch her own reflection in the glass. "I was leaving my doctor's office. I was twenty-two, and I'd just been tested for STDs, after being sexually assaulted."

Max made a sharp movement in his forgotten corner, but neither of the women looked at him.

"I was clean, but they told me I'd have to wait and be retested for HIV. I'd locked my keys in my car, and had to call a locksmith. The guy, when he showed up, was all smiles and flirting. It was like he had no idea where we were. And it was all I could do to respond, to even hear him when he spoke. I was dying on the inside, and he didn't even notice. Then when he was leaving, he told me to smile." Her bloody hands clenched together on the table top and Helena watched flakes crunch up and drift away.

"That's fucked up," said Max.

Sarah turned to look at him, offered another smile. "It

really is, isn't it?"

"Was that him tonight? The guy? Was he the one that told you that? Is that why?"

Helena sat forward, frowned at him.

"No," said Sarah, turning to face forward again. "No, that was decades ago. I still remember, though."

"So, what, then?" asked Helena. "What's the connection?"

Sarah shrugged. "The connection is simple. He said it to me tonight. I was walking home from the bus stop. It was cold, and I've been sick for a week. I was thinking about all the papers I had to grade, and the fact that I'll have to move my mom into assisted living soon. She's going to fight me on it, and I don't blame her, but she's broken her hip three times in as many years." She blew out a small breath. "Anyway. This guy, Kevin, he was leaving a convenience store, the one on the corner of Vine and Market?"

Helena nodded. She knew the one.

"And he just glanced at me, and told me to smile, it wasn't that bad." Her pale face scrunched up. "But it *was*. You know? It was."

"Yeah," Helena replied, her voice soft.

"So, I asked him to step up to my place. It was close, less than a block. I'm sure he thought he was about to get lucky, so he did. And then, when we got inside, I just..." Her voice faded. She dropped her gaze to her lap again.

Helena cleared her throat. "How?"

Sarah's brow wrinkled. "That's what I've been trying to remember. I've been looking at my hands, and thinking of ways I must have done it. But...I can't see it."

"What do you see?"

Sarah looked up, past Helena to the room's stark ceiling. "What is that? What's that song? I keep thinking I remember the name, the lyrics, but every time I try..."

"Sarah. What do you see?"

Her eyes found Helena's again. "I don't *see* anything. That's the trouble. It's what I hear. Like the psychic scream of every woman who's been told to smile through the pain. Not because it'll make things better for her, you know? But so her *face* doesn't bother the people around her."

Helena frowned, watching her. Because for a moment it was as though she heard that scream as well. Not here, not now, but ten years ago, feeling hope slide out of her in thick, dark gouts.

She stood, pushed away from the table. "We'll be back. Sit tight."

Sarah didn't seem to notice, staring at the ceiling again.

Max followed her out, and to the break room for coffee. He poured hers black, into the mug she liked. She went to the window, looked out into the night, smeared by too bright lights.

He moved to her shoulder, but not too close. Max was good with space bubbles.

"Pretty fucked up," he said.

"Which part?"

"All of it. What that guy said to her, back then. Right after...you know. And then tonight..." he cleared his throat. "Do you think it's...I mean, is it always that bad? Like, enough to kill for?"

Helena thought about it. Seeing her own reflection transposed across the dark, dirty night. "No. Most of the time it isn't, it's just annoying, and condescending. Like the guy telling me to smile while I'm working out. Fuck off, right? I'm benching 160, so spot me or move on." She took a breath. "But sometimes it hurts. Sometimes it's the last thing you need, and it's piled on top of a whole lot of other psychic baggage. The way our bodies are seen as out there for public consumption, commentary. Right down to the expression on our faces."

Max sipped his coffee. "I never thought about it that way. I always thought it was a douchey thing to do, but think of saying that to somebody on the worst day of their lives."

"Yeah." She frowned, tilted her head. "Tell me you hear that."

Max looked around. "The humming? Yeah, I think it's her." He jerked his head in the direction of Interview One, only a wall away from where they stood.

"You know the song?"

He frowned. "No, I can't quite...but it does seem familiar." He snapped his fingers.

"This turning into Westside Story?" snarked Bellows, edging in to get to the coffee. They both ignored him.

Phones began to ring all over the station. Dispatch lit up with a hundred calls, but Helena heard something else. A cry, of a hundred thousand voices at once. She winced, dropped her coffee, and slapped her hands to her head as the scream shivved into her frontal lobe. She saw a thousand faces, unsmiling, unhappy, hurting. Felt their hearts breaking as one.

Max was at her shoulder, saying something, asking what was wrong.

Bellows leaned against the table. "Smile, boss. It's not that bad."

The scream stopped. The pain went with it, but then another scream started. This one from deep in Bellows' throat. Helena watched, fascinated, as his eyes rolled back in his head, his mouth stretching impossibly wide. The skin strained, pulled tight. A nauseating crack as both jaws broke at once, and the man's face split from his lips back to his ears. The top of his head flipped open, like a mangled Venus fly trap. His scream tapered off into a gargle, then even that went silent as he slid to the floor.

"Jesus," said Max, retching beside her. "Jesus, what the fuck—"

The phones still rang. There were screams in the street below, but above it all, Helena heard singing. Maybe it was Sarah, or maybe it was only in her head, but it was a relief to recognize the song at last.

She looked into Bellows' esophagus, spurting blood, and wondered if he was finding life worthwhile.

HOOKING UP

"**H**as anyone ever told you you're beautiful?"

The intended compliment is accompanied by hovering proximity, and I feel the heat of his body, smell the overwhelming blast of body spray imperfectly concealing a whiff of sour sweat. His tone tells me he expects me to blush and modestly declaim. His expression is earnest, his mouth curved in a half-smile, his eyes soulful like he thinks he's Jordan Catalano.

I look him up and down, then return my attention to the action at the bar across the room. "Of course," I answer, chewing on the stem of a maraschino cherry steeped in the bourbon of my Old Fashioned.

He doesn't know what to do with that, so he moves to get my attention again. "You know," says Catalano wannabe, his eyebrow raised in what I soon realize is playful admonition. "Guys don't like it when girls think too much of themselves. Vanity's not attractive."

"Heavens," I say in my flattest tone. "Could you move? You're blocking my view."

He turns to see what's stolen my attention from him—not that it ever belonged to him in the first place—and is visibly nonplussed by the scene at the bar. He's expecting some pretty boy, or a muscled Adonis, because the only thing worth losing the attentions of a man is another man. He doesn't see what I see, and I don't pay him any more mind, so he pisses off. I've tuned him out so whatever snide comments he makes are lost to the thump of the bass.

I lean farther over the table I've staked out, twenty feet from the bar. Far enough so I'm hidden in shadow but close enough for regular refills from the bottle of Bulleit I'm planning to make a sizable dent in. I spit the mangled cherry stem into my glass and lick the juice from my lips, watching the tired byplay of the non-couple standing at the unoccupied end of the bar. Romeo and Juliet I've dubbed them, the names I always use when I watch one of these skirmishes. Juliet's broadcasting every sign of disinterest—her shoulders are up, tight, and one arm is crossed over her belly. The other clutches a nearly empty martini glass she keeps raising to her lips, then lowering. Her eyes scan the thin crowd of patrons, seeking respite from anywhere, but her friends must have found their own hookups and are nowhere to be seen. It hasn't occurred to her she can just leave. It never does.

Romeo's ignoring every one of her signals, leaning way into her space bubble, his grin fatuous and cocksure. A long neck of some watery brand of beer dangles from the fingers of one hand while the other rests on her hip, making playful climbs up her side. Once he even goes high enough to pull down the neckline of her top and peer at her breasts. That shocks her enough to pull away, but not to deliver the backhand he so richly deserves. He takes it as a joke, or pretends to, laughing and moving ever closer.

I'm a regular here, and I've seen this dance more times

than I can count. The result is almost always the same, so you might wonder why I keep coming back for more, but ask a die hard football fan of a piss poor team why they line up every Sunday for more punishment. Love of the game, and an immortal flame of hope.

"Come *on*," I mutter when Romeo moves close enough to press his crotch to her leg. "Tell him to fuck off."

He's rubbing his dick on her—surely that's enough to earn him a knee in the balls. I can almost see her skin crawling from where I sit, but other than a single step back she doesn't react to his lewd act. He's got a hard on that's visible from across the room, and I know it's going to take more gumption than she has to escape his clutches. To men like him, boners are an unbreakable promise.

I down the rest of my drink and make my way to the bar, stopping near Romeo and Juliet, my back to them but close enough to listen in. The bartender catches my eye and I raise my glass, hold up a finger. He nods and turns back to the wall of bottles.

"C'mon, let's get out here," Romeo says, his lips close to Juliet's ear, but the words are shouted to be heard over the music and she winces.

I've turned just enough so I can watch the action out of my peripheral vision, crunching bourbon-soaked ice while I wait.

"I really can't, not tonight," says Juliet. "Another time? I can give you my number."

She would, too, and it probably wouldn't even be fake. Push the problem off for another day and cringe every time her phone rings. I'm not judging, but I am rooting for her to find her spine and whack him over the head with it.

The bartender drops off my drink just as body spray guy reappears at my side. He raises an eyebrow and gives a half smile before telling the bartender to add it to his tab. Bartender looks at me and I shake my head, so he moves on to the next customer without taking Body Spray's order.

"So what's your poison?" he asks, moving too close so he can peer in my glass. "Red headed slut?"

I roll my eyes. "It's an Old Fashioned."

"An old fashioned what?" he asks, and he's not joking.

I sigh and turn my back on him, just in time to watch Romeo lead Juliet out of the bar by the hand. She's trailing two steps behind, dragging her feet like a recalcitrant toddler, but her obvious distaste hasn't been enough to spare her fate. I'm disappointed. I shake my head and down half my drink, fishing for the cherry with my tongue.

Body Spray moves around to my other side, leans an elbow on the bar and glances over his shoulder at the retreating couple. He looks back at me and grins. "They've got the right idea, you know. Night's young."

"But I'm not," I say, pushing away from the bar. He follows me. Not like a puppy, because puppies are fucking cute and who wouldn't want one ambling after them, all big paws and ears? No, this guy follows me like a strip of toilet paper, soiled and embarrassing and bizarrely hard to shake. Over the next half hour he won't leave my side, making every tired play in the book, and none of the right ones. I don't have vicarious entertainment anymore so I choose not to chase him off, but I don't give him any encouragement. In fact I'm rude as hell, rolling my eyes, letting my disdain drip from every pore, withholding a single word of acknowledgment, let alone interest.

In the space of those thirty minutes I order two more drinks, and Body Spray downs three beers and a few shots of rotgut tequila. Sweat beads on his brow and his upper lip. Maybe it's the alcohol, or maybe it's the thrill of grinding this guy under my heel, but warmth and a dull throb take up residence between my thighs. I'm done fucking around—I have an itch to scratch, and he's close to hand.

I toss off the rest of my drink, slam the glass down on the table beside me, and reach for his crotch. He's not expecting it, the feel of my hand clasping around his dick through his jeans momentarily robbing him of speech. He's hard almost instantly and pushes himself against my palm, teeth gritting.

"I knew it," he says in a breathy under voice, pressing closer and trying to wrap his arms around me, grab my ass.

"Not yet," I say, still holding his crotch, dodging his hands. "I want to get out of here first."

Before he can agree I head for the exit, leading him by the dick.

"Hey, I like where your mind's at but maybe you can hold onto something else while we're walking?" he asks, hurrying to stay close.

I don't look back at him, grabbing on tighter. "Keep up, or next time I'll go looking for a longer leash."

"Jesus," he says under his breath, anger cutting through the fog of alcohol, but only until I rub my thumb over him. His mouth opens, closes, then he's back to trotting in my wake, following his dick like he has his whole life.

We get out to the parking lot, weaving through a pack of drunks who don't feel the need to share the sidewalk. Body Spray is oblivious to their giggles and lewd comments until we're a few yards away and one of them yells.

"Yo Doug, don't forget to tip her!" calls a frat-bro-looking dude, none too steady on his feet.

Body Spray, or Doug, straightens up and tries to pull out of my grasp. "Hey, keep it a little cooler, okay?"

I ignore him. "Which one's yours?"

He hesitates but doesn't look back at the group who

have stopped to watch the show. Suddenly he cares about appearances, after trying all night to put his hands on me, but he's flipped my switch and I'm not giving up that easily. I rub my hand down to find his balls beneath the thick fabric of his jeans and cup them, my middle finger stroking the tender flesh beneath.

"Which one?" I ask again, my breath hot in his ear.

"The Jeep—that green one over there," he groans.

He tries to push me up against the door when we get there, hands going for my breasts, but I dodge again.

"I told you, not yet."

He stares blearily at me. "I thought you meant not in there."

"So you figured banging me in your backseat was sufficient? No wonder you're so desperate for action," I say, letting go of his crotch.

There's a catcall from the sidewalk, more use of his name. These people know him, no doubt, and that's a problem. For him, anyway.

He looks over his shoulder, licks his lips. "Look, we can't go back to my place. I've got roommates." He moves to hide his left hand, stuffing it in his pocket, but I could give a shit about the silver band I noted earlier in the evening. His marriage isn't my problem.

"Can't go back to my place, either," I say.

"Why?" he asks, grinding against me.

"Because I don't want you there."

He recoils for a few seconds, but again his libido overwhelms his pride. He leans closer, inexpertly kissing my neck and leaving saliva in his wake instead of goosebumps. "So what do you want?"

I sigh and press myself against him. "I want...to feel like a teenager again. All those hormones, back when I could make out with a guy for hours and not get tired of it. You know what I mean?"

He takes a step back and pushes his hair out of his eyes. "Uh, I don't know about hours. I hafta be up pretty early."

I pull back, hands at my sides, and shrug. "Okay, no problem. Some other time then." I turn my back and head in the direction of the bar.

He hesitates for less than a second before catching up and grabbing my arm. "C'mon, don't do that. We've got a connection—let's not waste it."

I don't turn back. "I'm not wasting anything."

He growls, sighs. "Okay, fine. You want a teenage makeout session? Let's do it." He checks for his friends then pulls me back into the shadowed parking lot, pushing me up against the Jeep again, hands going straight for my breasts.

I slap them down this time. "I told you, not yet. You gotta get me hot if you want any of this."

He pants, his sweat all over me by now. "You trying to tell me you're not hot for me? I don't buy that, babe." He reaches for the bottom of my skirt and this time I shove him, hard.

He's rounded the corner into pissed off by then, a locale he should have arrived at an hour ago. He glares at me, bleary red eyes narrowed, and his hands clench into fists.

"Oh, big tough guy, what do you think you can accomplish with those, anyway?" I ask, at the same time I pull my shirt down on the right side, enough to show a black satin bra, nicely filled out.

He bites back whatever he was going to say, some version of bitch or whore or tease. He looks over his shoulder, licks his lips. "There's a park near here—about a ten minute drive. It'll be deserted this time of night."

I press close to him again. "That's more like it," I say in

his ear, pulling away before he can touch me and making my way to the passenger seat.

He makes no effort to open the door for me, but that's not what I want from him, anyway. He climbs into the driver's seat and tries to kiss me again, so I turn away to look out the window.

"Drive," I say, my tone as bored as I can make it.

We're on the road less than a minute before his hand is in my lap, but I pick it up and put it back. "The way you rush everything, I'm starting to think this drive will last longer than your performance. Learn patience," I tell him, watching his fingers squeeze the wheel like he wants to do to me.

The car gets quiet except for road noise, and I watch the city lights disappear, the night impenetrable in a way it never is close to civilization. I look around and pull my seat belt tighter. "Are we almost there?" I ask, casting a glance at his profile.

He smirks. "What happened to your patience?"

When my only response is a flat stare, he shrugs. "Just a few more minutes." He looks over at me and his smile widens. "Getting nervous? Don't worry, I'll protect you."

I roll my eyes and make sure he can see it. "Oh, *now* I feel safe."

His lips purse and he grips the steering wheel again. "You'll be glad I'm there, believe me. It can get creepy out there."

"Creepier than in here?" I ask.

His jaw clenches. "Funny. If I'm such a creep, why're you in my car?"

I give him my sweetest smile. "Because you're easy."

Doug leans back in his seat, drives with only one hand. He doesn't say another word as we turn off the main drag and follow a circuitous path of ever narrower streets, finally grinding up a gravel path in total darkness. When he stops the Jeep, there's not a light for miles.

I peer into the night, noting the fog that's hovering low on the edges of the road. "This is your go-to romantic spot? How the hell did you get anyone to marry you in the first place?"

"I'm not—" he starts, but I cut him off.

"Of course you are. Don't disrespect her like that. You really suck at hiding it, but if I cared I wouldn't be here."

Doug's jaw is clenched, his brow stormy. "Marriage is bullshit, a societal construct. You want to know the truth, I felt sorry for her."

I snort. "Me, too, dude."

He's at least as angry as he is horny, and he makes sure I know it. He comes after me with rough kisses, his teeth grinding against my lips, squeezing my right breast viciously. I make no move to stop him—I like it like this.

Before we get too far, a sound comes from the roof of the car: a light tapping. He doesn't hear it at first but I put a hand on his chest, push him back.

"What was that?" I ask.

He looks up, shrugs. "Who cares? Probably just branches."

I look out the window into nothing. "Did we park under a tree?"

He doesn't bother to answer, trying instead to get my top off but I push it back down.

"Have you heard of the hook hand killer?" I ask, crossing my arms over my chest.

He gives a heavy sigh. "The incredibly generic urban legend? Yeah, everyone's heard that one." He reaches for me again but I pull back, swiveling in the seat to face him.

"No, not that one—I mean the real hook hand killer, the

one that's been operating for the last couple years. Supposed to have killed ten people."

He smirks, takes my hand and puts it on his crotch. "Don't worry—I said I'd protect you."

I glance down. "With *that*? You don't bring a knife to a sword fight."

His face goes red and he fumbles for his zipper. "Oh yeah?" He pulls his dick out through the front of his boxers and thrusts his hips forward. "Still think it's just a little knife?"

From his tone I'm supposed to be impressed, chagrined at maligning his package, but what he holds in his hand is just another dick. I twist my lips. "I didn't realize it was that cold in here."

Before he can answer I look outside again. "Now that hook hand guy—he's really exciting. He's hit six states and never come close to getting caught. Every victim cut ear to ear, starting right here, at the jaw." I run a finger along my jawline, dip it across my neck before cupping my breasts.

"That's what gets you off?" Doug says, stuffing himself back in his pants.

I shrug. "It's just exciting to think about. Kind of visceral, you know? Like telling a scary story around a campfire—it's a little thrill."

He grunts and turns away. "If you say so."

I punch his arm. "C'mon, where's your sense of fun?"

He raises his left hand without looking at me, taps the wedding band. "Fun went out the window a few years ago."

I snort, not even trying to make it cute. "Oh, please. The ball and chain routine? Is this a nineties sitcom?"

He slews his body around again, leans close into my space. "The fuck would you know about it, huh? Your idea of a good time is talking about murder? Bet you'd love it if I *was* the hook hand killer."

My heart freezing, I stare at him. "Are you?"

He licks his lips, looks me up and down. "Maybe I am. Maybe that's why I drove you all the way out here."

I stay motionless, watching him. "Maybe we should go back."

He grins and moves closer. "It's a little late for that."

The tapping comes again, from the hard top roof of the Jeep. It's louder this time and we both look up.

"Go see what it is," I hiss.

He laughs, a high, nervous sound. "As if. I'm not your fucking boyfriend—do it yourself."

I glare at him. "You're serious? Bragging all night about how you can protect me and you won't even go out and look?"

He peers through the windshield. "What's the point? There's nothing out there, anyway." He's trying to convince himself, and not succeeding.

I push him. "Real macho. Your friends know you're this weak?"

He's thinking of the buddies we ran into outside the bar, wondering whether I'll tell them. It almost gets him going, his fingers wrapped around the door handle, but a teeth grinding scratch comes from above and he jumps.

"Fuck, no," he says, voice shaking. "I'm not going out there."

I roll my eyes, nose wrinkling in disgust. "You really are worthless, aren't you? Fine, I'll do it."

He doesn't make a move to stop me, scrunched up as far away as he can get from the door I'm about to open. I hesitate, peering through the fog that's risen to window level since we've been here. I can't see a damn thing, but the scratching comes again. I throw the door open. "Pansy ass," I fire off before stepping outside. I turn, put my hand under my left breast where a gleaming silver hook curls beneath. A hook

I've used many times, that's as hungry as I am.

I don't get a chance to pull it before something comes at us, high speed and heavy, whistling in the wind. It thrusts through the windshield and I throw my arm up to save my eyes from flying glass. There's a thick, wet crunching noise and something warm spatters my arm. When I look again, there's a sword piercing my date's skull, impaling it to the headrest of his seat. I get a good look at it: a thick, sharp blade entering through Doug's right eye, brain matter leaking out the exit wound. He's still moving, still making noise, but it's just reflex—it'll be over soon.

He leans forward and I flinch back, almost falling out the open door. I slam it quickly closed behind me and see Doug isn't moving of his own volition: the sword is being slowly retracted, making a screeching sound against the glass as it does. The blade gets stuck on its way out of Doug's face, and he's slammed several times against the broken windshield, blood smearing and leaking into the cracks with each impact. Finally it pulls free and he slumps forward, head landing on the steering wheel.

I fumble with the lock to my own door, but the driver's side opens wide, fog rolling in. An enormous, gloved hand reaches in and pulls the dead man from the car, his body landing in the gravel below with a meaty thud. A huge hooded shadow looms, watching me from hidden eyes before climbing into the vacated seat.

He doesn't look at me, but I look at him. I study the brown gloves he wears—they look like falconer gloves. His hoodie is a nondescript gray, his jeans are filthy. The sword leans against the open door but he doesn't reach for it, or me.

We sit like that for seconds that feel like minutes. My breath coming fast, I'm frozen with indecision—the creep's immobility warding off any sudden movements. Why the fuck is he here? Why isn't he talking?

When he finally opens his mouth it's not what I'm expecting. A reedy, breathless voice at odds with the man's size, and nothing he says is normal.

"Hell is the absence of God," he intones. "Dark is the absence of light."

I stare at him, no idea where this is going.

"What absence defines me?" he continues, not looking at me. "What crucial element missing from my soul is what makes me, me, and not someone else? Whatever it is, I don't feel its loss—there is no emptiness inside me, waiting to be filled. I am complete exactly as I am, and define myself anew whenever I please."

He stops there, and after a bit it feels like he's expecting an answer.

"Okay?" I say. "That doesn't explain what you're doing in my car."

He shakes his head. "Not your car."

"And how do you know that?" I ask.

"I watched you. In the bar."

"Tonight?" I frown.

"Lots of nights."

There's a greasy roil in my gut, thinking of this guy stalking me night after night, and me seeing nothing. What an idiot—no better than Juliet, oblivious to what's really happening.

"You didn't feel me?" he asks, finally turning to look at me, but his hood and the darkness keep his face in shadow. All I can see is a nose, fleshy and canted to the side.

"Feel you?" I ask, distracted.

"Humans," says the killer, his voice throbbing with revulsion, "have a built-in detector for psychopaths. An eerie feeling, hairs standing up on their arms, anxiety in their bellies when they sense one behind them. It's nature's way of telling them to flee, like the prey they are. You've never felt that?"

"No," I say, wrenching my gaze away to face front, studying the way Doug's smeared blood shades the cracked glass a glistening pink.

I jump when he claps his hands together, crowing before he leans close enough for me to smell the mint on his breath.

"I knew it. You're one of us—psychos don't trigger the same reaction in each other."

I look back at him. "You're calling me a psycho?"

His hood slides back far enough for me to see his mouth, grinning in the dark. "You knew what you were doing in there. You're the same as me. Guys like him," he says, inclining his head to where Doug lies bleeding on the gravel path, "always want the same, dirty thing. The world's a better place without them, but it takes a special kind of person to be a hunter. I knew when I saw you—you're that kind of person."

I stare at him for the space of several thudding heartbeats before I reach behind and unlock my door, fling it open and step into the night. I don't get far—he's climbed out and circled around the hood before I can go two steps. We stop, sizing each other up.

"Don't bother running, I can catch you. And don't waste your time screaming."

Adrenaline spikes my blood pressure, but outwardly I'm calm. "I'm not a screamer," I say.

He gives a deep chuckle and takes another step closer. "Of course you're not. Like I said, you're one of us."

The thought revolts me—I'm nothing like this cretin, but there's no point in arguing with a sick mind. I have to get away from this guy. I reach for my shirt, pull it down on the left side.

He stumbles backward, raising a hand in front of his

eyes. "No, don't do that. We're beyond those kinds of urges—what we have is pristine, pure."

He stops talking when my hook punctures the soft meat under his jaw, slicing up far enough to nail his tongue to the roof of his mouth. He fights me, thinking he can use his size to his advantage, but my arm holds steady. I've had lots of practice.

Blood pools and slips from between lips he cannot open to scream, or speak, but I see the question in eyes grown desperate.

"You want to know why?"

He doesn't dare to nod, but I push the hook further anyway. It punctures his palette and his body shudders, tears squeezing from his eyes.

"There *is* no why," I hiss, getting in his face. "There's no punishment—you think that's why I'm here? There's no morality to murder. Body Spray over there's a douche, but that doesn't mean I'm serving up justice. The world is arbitrary and dark and cruel, and I'm part of it." I lean close enough for my lips to brush his cheek. "And for the record? That whole 'women are psycho' bit is fucking archaic. Label yourself if you want, but every throat I cut is a choice." I jam the hook the rest of the way into his brain and he jitters on the end of it, the blood flowing fast and gloving my hand in crimson. I watch the light go from his eyes, and I sigh. I've been waiting for this release all night, and I relish it, riding the wave to its completion.

I yank my hook from his gullet with a gristly squelch and wipe it on his hoodie as he topples to the ground, dead weight no longer supported by the upward pressure of my arm. I tuck the hook back in my bra where it curls nicely at the bottom of my breast. Looking around at the carnage, I'm irritated all over again. Legends vary, they take their own shape in the telling and retelling, but this scene is chaos. There's nothing for it, I'll have to retire the hook hand killer. I hate that—the hook is convenient, versatile. I've gotten comfortable with it, but maybe that's the problem. I let Doug's friends see me, back at the bar, so it's time to move on, anyway. I'm going to miss that bartender.

I crunch down the long gravel drive lost in thought, wondering how to remake myself, which legend to subsume next. I've always liked Bloody Mary, but it's too passive a role. I don't want to wait to be conjured. I step out onto the main road and turn in the direction of town, and the bar where my car waits. I'd love to take Doug's Jeep and spare myself the effort, but that would only lead to more questions. I haven't been walking long when a sedan pulls up beside me, a middle-aged man with glasses and a weak chin leaning out the lowered window.

"You need a ride, missy? Too late to be out here by yourself—all kinds of things go on at that lover's lane a ways back."

I bend over and look into his car. He's the only one inside. I smile, feeling myself change to meet this new challenge.

"Thanks," I say, and climb inside, knowing where I'm headed next.

VIGNETTES OF WOMANHOOD

BULLET PROOF

She heads into a war zone every day. No hazard pay, but the risks are high and her armor is flimsy. Masks and sanitizing wipes she buys herself because there's little more than shrugs and patronizing shoulder pats from the people who should know better. There was a time she thought adults knew what they were doing, that administrators took careful inventory and made thoughtful decisions. She knows now that she is the only thing standing between her students and the possibility of something very bad. Today it is disease, but yesterday it was bullets.

She has her own child at home, splits her time and headspace between being the best mom, and the best teacher. No room left in there for just being her.

"Take it easy," they tell her. "You can't save the world."

Perhaps not, but neither can she stop trying.

THE GOODBYE HOUSE

Sabrina didn't advertise The Goodbye House. Never spoke of it to her hospice patients or their families, nor even those more closely connected to her who'd lost loved ones and might be looking for a second chance. It didn't work like that—people had to find their own way to the two-story, German-style Tudor. Otherwise the magic didn't happen, the portals and vessels that lined the rows of tables and filled the shelves standing against each wall staying closed and silent.

In the early days, the items, the goodbyes as she came to call them, were a modest collection covering only the surface of a coffee table display she kept in the living room. Small knickknacks: compacts, miniature bibles, drink coasters, carvings. None of them valuable, nothing that would be missed. Some of them taken from the dressers and nightstands of the people who died under her watch, but not all. At first she'd felt guilty about that—she never took jewelry or photos, but you never knew what might hold sentimental value for someone. People channeled a lot of their grief into physical objects, which was at least half the reason for the brutal battles over inheritances she'd witnessed. But certain things called to her, once the person crossed over. A playing card, an arrowhead, a matchbook. She came to believe it was the spirit guiding her choice, but it was rare for that goodbye to belong to the recently departed from whom she took it. Proximity and ownership had no bearing, and she found, over time, that browsing a pawn shop or a yard sale could yield effective results. She learned to recognize a faint sheen, a shimmer like the air over a flame, and when she traced her fingers over the item's surface, she could feel the touch of other hands. These were the live ones, unused, a goodbye still waiting inside.

As the years went by, either her skill at recognition grew or the goodbyes learned to find her. Sometimes strangers pressed objects into her palm, a faraway look in their eye. Other times she would reach into her purse and close her fingers around something that hadn't been there before, smooth and warm, or cool and rough, waiting to join the other goodbyes. Maybe it was stealing—Sabrina had no memory of taking these items, and she certainly hadn't paid for them. But she assuaged her conscience with the knowledge that the goodbyes were being put to the best possible use.

She'd seen it far too often in hospice work—people tortured over the last exchanges they had with someone who'd died, attaching too much importance to an arbitrary time frame. Letting it consume them, riddle them with guilt, taint their memories, as though the sum total of their relationship, a lifetime of love—or whatever their connection to the deceased—could be negated by fumbling that last bit at the end. She made it a point to give people their privacy when they came looking, but she'd seen the peace it brought, when they left The Goodbye House without the burden of guilt they'd brought with them. It was better than any payment she'd been offered over the years. She didn't accept money—

she was a facilitator, nothing more. A higher power led her to the goodbyes, and that same power brought her the people that needed them.

Friday had been a good day. She didn't have to work, had no patients for the next two days. Weekends off were a rarity, since death didn't recognize business hours, and she'd been glad for the break. The weather was finally turning, the bite of winter giving way to spring breezes, the windows open on the second floor. She'd had two callers, a young man in his twenties and a woman in her sixties, both weighted by grief, unsure how they'd ended up at her door.

They always had that look—lips parted, a fist held at their chest, as though they hadn't meant to knock. Bewildered, a little lost, but willing enough when she invited them inside. The house was old, early 1900's, the ceilings high and airy. Big windows with the original glass intact let in sunlight to dapple the oak floors. There was a spiral staircase to the left, but most people were drawn forward, to the open rooms where the goodbyes waited. She would walk them to where the tables and shelves began, then leave them be while they searched.

It usually didn't take long. By the time someone made their way to Sabrina, their hearts were open to the experience. They knew on a subconscious level who they were there for. She'd learned not to assume her visitors were dealing with a recent loss—that had been a holdover from some quaint idea of unfinished business. The goodbyes were about the living, not the dead, and the folks left behind could carry a hurt for decades. There had been one man, well into his eighties, who'd refused to tell his father goodbye when the man lay dying, over half a century before. Sabrina hadn't pried into the reasons—plenty of family deserved that kind of treatment, and her only concern was the seeker before her. He'd taken a little longer than most, but in the end, he found his goodbye, and left with tears streaming down his creased, smiling face.

There had been nothing out of the way about her two visitors that day—the young man had been missing his mother, and the woman was looking for a dear friend she hadn't known had passed until months after the fact. They'd found what they were looking for, the young man stopping to crush Sabrina in a hug before he left, and she was warmed by the same feeling of peace and accomplishment she got after every goodbye. She'd made her way through the tables and quickly found the two items that had emptied out—an ornate glass ashtray and a wooden pencil. Both had fulfilled their purposes and were nothing more than inert objects now, so she'd wrapped them in newspaper and packed them into an open box. They were just things now, of no particular value or use, but it felt wrong throwing them out, so she never did. One of these days she was going to run out of space.

As daylight faded, she made popcorn and curled up on the sofa to watch a true crime show, but the opening sequence hadn't even finished when she heard a noise at her door. She sat up and paused the television, holding her breath and listening. The noise came again, a scratching that was too rhythmic to be anything but intentional. *Shave and a haircut...* The most common knock in the country, but who scratched at a door like that?

Sabrina rose and cast a glance behind her, at the darkened house full of waiting goodbyes. She knew this would be about them, but the open second floor windows made her feel cold, exposed. She set her bowl of popcorn down on the coffee table, wiped her hands on her sweat pants, and moved to the door. She wasn't going to open it—good deed or not, she didn't have to make The Goodbye House available at all hours. Whoever it was could come back tomorrow.

"Hello?" came a voice from the other side of the door. Female, high pitched, a quaver at the end.

Sabrina frowned and stepped closer. "It's late," she said. "Come back tomorrow."

"Please." The voice got smaller. "I've come a long way."

Sabrina moved silently and stood on tiptoe to press her eye to the spyhole. The porch was dark, and she could make out little detail, but there was a diminutive woman standing there, her face in shadow, hands clasped in front of her.

Sabrina sighed. She'd never questioned why the machinations that guided The Goodbye House kept strangers from her door after nightfall, but over time, she'd taken it as a given. She didn't want to open the door, didn't want a stranger in her home just now, but people found their way here for a reason. She supposed the woman wouldn't have come if she wasn't supposed to.

"All right," she said. She eased the door open and tried to make out her visitor's face, but it was still obscured. She stepped aside, trying to reassert her usual personae. It was on the tip of her tongue to ask the woman to make it quick, but she reminded herself it wasn't a store at closing time. Goodbyes shouldn't be rushed.

"Thank you so much. I'm Elena," said the woman in a breathless voice, wobbly with tears.

Sabrina's frown deepened. No one introduced themselves at The Goodbye House. She hadn't given much thought to that, either, but she felt an intense aversion to sharing her name with the woman. "Hello, Elena."

Both women waited in the dim hall, Sabrina wrapping her arms around her middle. Elena looked around, stepping forward to peer up the staircase, light finally falling on her face. Sabrina studied her profile, the slender neck and soft jawline. Watery, pale blue eyes and a reddened nose. She looked to be much Sabrina's own age—mid fifties, but oddly fragile. Sabrina had grown used to thinking of herself as sturdy as she aged, enjoying the confidence that came with experience. Elena gave the impression she might fly apart at a touch. Sabrina allowed herself to relax—this woman was no danger to her.

Ingrained upbringing finally made her break the silence. "Are you ready?" she asked.

Elena turned to her, the full force of those wide open eyes focused on Sabrina. Elena's lipstick was a vibrant orange-red, drawn well outside the lines of her mouth, lips dry and flaking. "Ready for what?" she asked, her voice even smaller, with a babyish tone. No, more like how adults sounded when they tried to imitate children.

Sabrina's gaze narrowed, the discomfort returning to settle in her belly. She cleared her throat. "Don't you know why you're here?"

The other woman gave a slow, exaggerated head shake, lips folding, eyebrows up.

Sabrina bit her lip. This had never happened before. "Do you at least know who you're here for?"

A gleam came into Elena's eye, the corners of her orange mouth lifting. "I'm here for someone?"

Sabrina looked behind Elena at the closed front door. For the first time she wished her little hobby had come with instructions, or a help line. This didn't feel right, and prompting the woman to give the right answers went against everything she thought she knew about The Goodbye House. But she couldn't explain what it was about the other woman that got her back up, made her want to shove her back on the porch and lock every door and window.

She took a deep breath, assumed a gentle smile. "How did you come to be here, Elena?"

Elena didn't answer for several seconds, then her eyes slid from Sabrina's and she returned her attention to the staircase, going so far as to take another step toward it. The second floor belonged to Sabrina alone; no one else ever went up there. No one else had ever tried. Sabrina stepped in front of her.

"Elena? If you don't know why you're here, how come you came such a long distance, and knocked on a stranger's door at night?"

Elena pursed her thin lips. "I don't know, I guess someone told me about this place. That I should come here, and it would help me. Fix me." Tears welled in her eyes and her lips trembled.

Sabrina's ready sympathy swelled. She put a hand on the other woman's arm. "I understand. Grief can make it seem like everything in your life is broken, can't it?"

Elena gave a vigorous nod, tears shaking loose to streak mascara down her cheeks. She clamped a hand over Sabrina's, locking it in place. "It really can. You're the first person to say that to me, to understand." The tears came faster and she gave a snort-sniff that turned Sabrina's stomach.

Sabrina pulled her hand loose with effort and went to the living room to get the woman a box of tissues. When she turned around Elena was right behind her, peering at the paused screen of the television, eyes traveling over the cluttered coffee table and half-full bowl of popcorn.

"I love that show," she said brightly. "It's my favorite." She watched Sabrina in expectant silence.

Sabrina lifted a shoulder. "It's okay."

Elena immediately shook her head. "Yeah, exactly, not as good as some of the other ones. Which one is *your* favorite?"

Sabrina pushed the tissue box into her hand and guided her back to the main hall. "I think it's time, don't you?"

Elena looked at her. "Time for what? Oh, please don't make me go yet. This is the first time I've felt okay in *ages*. It's people, you know. I'm not good with them, always manage to mess things up, but you're so open, so easy to talk to."

Warning bells sounded in every corner of Sabrina's mind, but she made herself quiet them. This woman was in a bad place, needed a friend, so she'd turned to the nearest polite stranger. Even so, she couldn't stay all night. Sabrina took Elena by the elbow and brought her to the first room of goodbyes, hoping the pull of whoever she was there to see would override everything else.

"This is why you're here," she said, and let go of Elena's arm.

Elena looked around, her gaze taking in the tall shelves, the tables, all the goodbyes. "Wow," she said. "What is all this stuff?"

Sabrina knew she shouldn't do it, but she needed to nudge this lady out the door. "They're the goodbyes."

Elena looked at her. "Goodbyes?"

Sabrina nodded. "Each one is a chance to say goodbye, to someone outside our reach."

A strange gleam came into the other woman's pale eyes and the corners of her clown's mouth lifted. "Anyone? I can use them to talk to *anyone*?"

Sabrina frowned. "Not exactly. It's not like a phone card, it's just a chance to make things right. Say what needed to be said, and find some peace."

Elena's smile widened, she looked back at the hundreds of goodbyes in the first room. "How many do I get?"

Sabrina opened her mouth but was silenced when a rush of air went through the room, stirring the pages of an open bible, ruffling the loose hairs around her face. It was cold, and somehow heavy, and when it was gone the room felt airless, confined.

Elena hadn't noticed, was still watching Sabrina with that oddly wide smile.

Sabrina shook her head. "Only one. Everyone gets one— the one person that's weighing on your heart."

Grayish teeth appeared over Elena's bottom lip. "And this time he'll have to listen."

Sabrina stared at her, the hairs rising on the back of her neck. She should have listened to her instincts, not let this woman inside. Whoever she was, she hadn't come for a goodbye. But now that she was here, Sabrina didn't know how to get rid of her short of bodily force. She just had to hope Elena would find what she was looking for and get out.

She chose not to answer, instead backing out of the room. "I'll be waiting in the front when you're finished."

She didn't turn her back on the woman, keeping an eye on her until she rounded the corner out of sight. She let out a breath, relieved to be out of proximity, but worry clenched her belly. Would Elena steal the goodbyes? Sabrina had never had to worry about such a thing—nothing in there held value beyond its capacity for final communication.

This time he'll have to listen...

For the first time she thought how tantalizing it might be for someone who didn't understand how The Goodbye House worked. Could a person force communication on a spirit who didn't want it? She thought of the old man who had taken decades to find enough inner peace to say goodbye to his father. What if the situations were switched and the son had died first? Could the father have coerced a goodbye from his deceased son? It was a stomach turning thought. Some hurts survived long past death.

She listened hard, hearing only slow steps in the other room, picturing Elena stopping and studying goodbyes as she went. Sabrina's heart pounded, her stomach roiling with apprehension. Would she have to force the woman out? Search her for stolen goodbyes? Wrestle a portal away from her to protect the eternal rest of someone who'd left Elena far behind?

All at once Elena's tread became swift and steady, and she appeared around the corner before Sabrina could move. Sabrina fought the urge to apologize for spying—this was her house after all, and she had a responsibility to it.

"All set?" she asked, scanning the other woman for bulging pockets or hands hidden behind her back.

Elena smiled. "Uh huh. Found what I was looking for, all taken care of. I'll be going."

They stared at one another for several beats, and Sabrina thought she'd never seen anyone so unaffected by a goodbye. She knew Elena was lying, but her hands were open and empty, her pockets flat. Sabrina wasn't going to strip search the woman, so instead she walked her to the door, glad to see the back of her.

Elena turned when she reached the porch and Sabrina braced herself. This was like the false ending of a slasher movie, where the lone, hidden survivor thinks the killer is leaving, then they turn and wreak havoc.

Instead, Elena offered another wide, orange smile. "Thank you *so* much for your help. I feel lots better."

Sabrina only gave a tight nod before closing the door and engaging every lock. She watched through the spyhole until Elena was out of sight, having half expected her to steal around the side of the house and come back. But she kept walking, finally becoming a dark smudge beneath a streetlight, and Sabrina allowed herself to breathe.

She hurried to the first room of goodbyes, searching for any gaps or used up items, but there was nothing. She checked the second room as well, then both again more slowly, but couldn't find an empty goodbye. Fine, that just confirmed her suspicion that Elena had lied.

"Sorry about that," she murmured to the rooms. "I'll be more careful in the future."

There was no answer. Sabrina hadn't expected one, but she didn't like the closed off, silent feel that hadn't been there before. She peered closer at a small wire hanger that rested on the table at hip level, but she could still see that sheen that told her a goodbye waited inside. She took another quick look around, then remembering the open windows upstairs, she hurried to close them.

It didn't make her feel better. Neither did checking all the doors and windows downstairs, or doing a quick search of the entire house. It felt as though the sanctity of The Goodbye House had been spoiled, and unease settled around her in the dark. She tried to finish her television show, but she couldn't concentrate; that sick rush of adrenaline kept returning. Elena's face would pop into her mind, and she'd jerk, her heart pounding, chest tight. She argued with herself each time—what exactly had the woman done? What harm had she caused? Sabrina's feelings weren't justified, she could see that, but she couldn't stop them, either.

Finally, she decided to head upstairs to her sanctuary. She realized as she took a final look around the ground floor that part of what was bothering her was the feeling of being alone. It was true she was always alone in the house—she hadn't lived with anyone since moving out of her mother's place at eighteen—but there was usually the comforting presence of the goodbyes, only a room away. She'd never thought of them as being possessed of life, or even a spirit's essence—they were just a touchstone, a gateway. But tonight it felt like whatever doors might lie within the myriad objects were closed tight against her.

Sabrina stood in the middle of the second room of goodbyes, scanning again for any that felt wrong or different. But it was all of them and none of them. She was about to go upstairs when she caught swift movement in the surface of a tiny framed mirror sitting high up on a shelf.

Sabrina's breath hitched in her chest and she looked behind her for whatever had caused the reflection. There was nothing, and no one. Her heart still pounding, she stood on tiptoes to take the mirror down.

She felt the familiar touch back of a charged goodbye when her fingers brushed the mirror's surface. It was a warm feeling, one of connection. She brought the mirror down to eye level and was faced with her own reflection.

Except...

Those weren't her eyes, she realized with a start. It was her mouth, her nose and chin, but the eyes that stared back at Sabrina were brown instead of her own hazel, somehow more masculine, and they were filled with a deep sadness.

Sabrina stared into them, her mouth parted. "Who—" she began, but cut off when she caught sight of movement in the mirror again. The stranger's eyes widened, and Sabrina turned, but she barely managed a glimpse before a shock of pain exploded from the base of her skull. She staggered, put her free hand to her head, touching warm blood soaking into her hair. Another blow fell, catching her hand and crushing it against her skull. She slumped to the floor, the mirror sliding from numb fingers.

"I'm just asking for an explanation. After all the time we spent together, all I gave up for you, you owe me that much."

Something clattered to the floor next to Sabrina's aching head. She squeezed her eyes shut against the nausea trying to creep its way up her throat. She didn't have the luxury of disorientation—she recognized the voice that was coming from somewhere above her. Elena had come back.

A thud vibrated through the hardwood floor and jarred Sabrina's splitting skull. She risked slitting one eye open, and once her vision cleared, she could make out a shadow moving erratically a few feet away. She closed her eyes again as a shower of lightweight objects scattered beside her—Elena must have whipped them all off at once.

"I know you can hear me."

Sabrina froze, her heart seizing, until the woman spoke again.

"That fat lady said everyone gets one goodbye, from the person that weighs heaviest. Well, that's you. I never got my goodbye, which was the *least* you could do. You know how hard things are for me, that I'd been hurt before. *Everybody* ends up hurting me, and I made you promise, the first time you kissed me, to never, ever do it. You were supposed to be the one that made up for all the others, but then you just *left.*"

The woman's voice caught on a sob, and Sabrina could tell by the fast, gulping sound of it that Elena was working herself into a fit. She swept more goodbyes from the shelves, picking up an old teacup and dashing it to the floor where it shattered, a bit of porcelain stinging as it nicked Sabrina's forehead. She stared at the broken goodbye, tears starting to pool in her eyes. Was that someone who had lost their chance? A mourner who would never find their way to peace, because the woman who'd broken into Sabrina's home couldn't take no for an answer?

She risked opening both eyes, looking around for anything she could use as a weapon. She couldn't let Elena destroy The Goodbye House. She couldn't let her torment some poor spirit. She didn't know if the contact could be forced, but even the chance of that kind of spiritual slavery was unconscionable.

"Where *are* you?" Elena seethed from the opposite corner. "I want my goodbye! I want you to tell me you're sorry, and you miss me, and you were wrong. I want to know you're suffering." The last word came out as a rage filled growl, followed by laughter that would have been jovial in any other setting.

Sabrina could see nothing that would help her. Nothing in the goodbye rooms was very heavy, or sharp. Her best chance was to get to the living room before Elena caught up with her and clock the bitch with a fireplace poker. She could probably get there in time if she could keep her head from swimming—Elena had only gotten the best of her before by sneaking up on her. She must have climbed through one of the windows before Sabrina had closed them—it was the only thing she could think. It wasn't important now: she needed to concentrate on surviving.

Her left hand grew warm all at once, and she almost jerked away, fearing she must have urinated on herself. But when her fingers moved, they brushed the mirrored surface of the goodbye she'd been holding when Elena struck her. She felt that touch back again, the urgent press of fingers from the other side. She closed her hand over the mirror and pulled it close to her body. Heat flared again.

She took a deep breath, clutched the mirror tight, and pushed to her knees. The next step would have been to lurch to her feet, but a wave of dizziness knocked her back, vomit spattering the floor in front of her. She couldn't stop her stomach's spasming, at long last wrenching a breath into her lungs. When she could see again, Elena stood before her, eyes narrowed, lips pursed and shaking with rage that was all out of proportion to the situation.

"You're keeping him from me, aren't you?" she asked, voice quivering, coming from the depths of the small woman's body like it was being dragged from her. "Are you working together? Behind my back, making sure I don't get my goodbye, my peace? Is that about the size of it?" Elena's voice rose with each punctuation until she was shouting in Sabrina's face.

There was a deeply ingrained part of Sabrina that wanted to calmly refute what the woman was saying. She didn't speak to the ghosts that came for their goodbyes. She didn't know any of their identities, or anything about them or the seekers who came to The Goodbye House. Even having dealt with people like Elena, Sabrina had never been able to rid herself of the conviction that it was her responsibility to fix the situation, to make the other person see the truth, not to acquit herself, but to ease their mental distress. She took one look at Elena's rabid expression and knew it was a lost cause. Instead she pushed to her feet, the mirror hidden behind her back, and took a lunging step toward Elena before pivoting and running for the other door. The lower floor of The Goodbye House was one big circle, each room leading into the next. She'd be able to get to the living room and a nice cache of makeshift weapons, if only she could keep moving.

Dizziness kept her vision and balance off kilter and the sudden movements made her stomach lurch again, but she bounced off the wall and kept her footing, telling herself puking while running wasn't the worst thing that could happen to her. Each time she almost fell the mirror flared again, the heat giving her focus, keeping her on track. She made it to the living room, her vision tunneled only on what she needed, the rack of fireplace tools that sat next to the brick base. Chest and stomach heaving, she reached for the poker, the most effective implement of destruction. Her free hand closed on the cold iron handle and she juggled the mirror to the crook of her arm so she could grasp the poker with both hands.

She heard running footsteps in front of her and focused her vision by sheer force of will. Elena stood before her, fury twisting her features, orange-red lipstick smeared across her bared, gray teeth. Sabrina didn't understand why the other woman looked so triumphant, until her gaze followed flickering light to Elena's outstretched hand. There was a goodbye in it, an old, forgotten corn husk doll Sabrina had found in the musty corner of a used bookstore. Its skirt was on fire, the dry materials burning swiftly, and Elena brandished the thing, firelight reflected in her too wide eyes.

"Give it to me," she hissed, her other hand held out, beckoning for what she thought belonged to her.

Sabrina blinked. "That thing'll burn out in another ten seconds. Fuck off."

Elena grabbed for a stick of firewood, dry from months of sitting in a basket, unused, the act of building a fire too much for Sabrina to contend with after nights spent with the dying. It lit quickly, carrying the torch as the cornhusk doll burned her last, and Elena held the flame close to the curling fringe of the rug.

"Give it to me, or I'll burn the whole place down."

The creepiest part was how calm Elena's voice got. She looked at Sabrina with clear eyes, her expression even. None of that meant she could be reasoned with, that she wouldn't torch the whole house just to get what she wanted.

Sabrina looked at the mirror in her hand. She saw those eyes again, sad and desperate. She thought of all those goodbyes stacked in two rooms, hundreds, thousands of chances for redemption, at risk because this woman couldn't understand. She thought of all the peace The Goodbye House had brought, all those smiling faces and hugs as people left their burdens with her. Was their happiness worth a few moments of unease for a man long dead? Her fingers loosened on the mirror, her hand drifted in Elena's direction.

Then she remembered how she'd gotten here. Litigating her own feelings, arguing against her discomfort because the evidence didn't seem to support it. She didn't understand how the spirit in the mirror ended up being dependent on her, at the mercy of someone like Elena. Maybe it meant she'd been wrong about the nature of The Goodbye House all along. It was impossible to know. But if there was the slightest chance she'd participated in coercing the dead, Sabrina knew she had to make up for it.

She drew back, held the mirror to her chest with one hand. "Then do it," she said.

Elena's face contorted. "Do you think I fucking *won't?* Give him to me. I need to know why. I need to understand, to hear his explanation." Her expression crumpled, tears flowing again. "Can't you understand that? It's the least he can do. I can't move on, can't be okay until he makes me understand."

Sabrina straightened her shoulders, took one last look around her home, and side-stepped Elena, giving the fire a wide berth.

"Get back here, you fat bitch! I'll do it, I'll fucking do it!"

"I have no doubt," Sabrina said without turning around. She found her purse near the front door and slung it over her shoulder. The only thing she took from The Goodbye House, besides the very last goodbye.

There were more words, more epithets, the kind people fell back on the instant their wills were crossed. Sabrina had learned long ago to stop paying attention, though it only enraged Elena more. She grasped at Sabrina with her free hand, clawing at her arm, her shoulder, her scalp, but Sabrina kept going, eyes front, back straight. It cost her a pang to step over the threshold for the last time—she'd been happy here, but she could no longer be certain she'd been humane. She knew what it was to be trapped. She'd never let it happen again.

She drove a safe distance before stopping to watch her home burn. Sabrina called emergency services after enough time had passed, and firetrucks streaked past her on their way to contain the blaze. She was glad—she wouldn't have wanted anyone else's home to catch fire.

She'd never doubted Elena's commitment to burning everything down in the quest to get her way, and she never saw the other woman leave. Maybe she had, sneaking out the back to avoid detection. Or maybe she'd died for her cause. It didn't really matter. For better or worse, the goodbyes were gone, swirling into the atmosphere, lost to unreasonable fury. Maybe they were glad to be free.

GHOSTED

This house is not haunted, no matter what you hear. At night by yourself, the echo in this empty chamber is your own, coming back to your ears in unfamiliar tones. It doesn't surprise me that you don't recognize it. That's probably not how it sounded in your head.

The creak on the steps behind you as you carry groceries to the kitchen—that's not me. It's just where you think I should be.

The door swinging open in slow motion while you hold your breath—I'm not behind it. Whatever the symbolism, the doors between us in my realm stay closed. I like it that way. And the phone calls with no one on the other end? The hissing silence that hints at a larger, darker realm beyond? Unknown caller, coming from inside your heart.

The séance is an invitation I do not accept—questions asked, is someone here—all signs point to no. The fingers on the planchette are yours and no one else's. I am not in the darkness beyond the circled light in which you sit.

I have no unfinished business; any need for closure is

your own. It's hard to live without answers, to sit graveside at our friendship and ask what happened, silence the only response. Tempting to assign an otherworldly explanation to this rift that, at long last, means more to you than it does to me. Because for the first time, I am the one with an earthly presence. No longer do I roam unseen, unheard, an unperson. I went into the light, one I made myself, and I am happy, my mourning done.

It's only ghosting because you never heard me in the first place. I haunted you then, but not anymore.

This house is clean.

SOMEONE HAS
TO DO IT

"Nellie. She's here."

Nell rolled to her back, pushed the hair out of her eyes. She'd squinted at the time on her phone before answering—not quite five a.m. Greg's hissed whisper didn't make any sense.

"Who's there?" she whispered back, though there was no one to worry about waking on her end.

"*Her.* Jessica. She's...she's back."

Nell sat up, the groggy haze of early morning gone as quick as that. Her big brother sounded...scared?

"Greg, you're having a dream. Sleep walking or something."

"I'm not walking, I'm talking, and I'm telling you I'm awake. And dead sober, in case that was your next guess."

It had been, so at least he'd saved her a step. Didn't mean she believed him. She took a breath and let it out slow, starting with the obvious. "Greg. That's not possible. Jessica's dead. The funeral was Sunday."

There was the start of a hysterical laugh, cut off before it could get out of control. "Fucking duh, Nell. You think I'd be calling my sister at the ass crack of dawn if it wasn't a fucked up situation?"

Nell scrubbed a hand over her face, swung her legs over the side of the bed and planted her feet on the floor. "Okay, let's back up. Tell me what you saw."

"I saw *her*. Jessica." His voice broke on his wife's name, as it had whenever he'd spoken it since the car accident.

"Saw her like a ghost, you mean? You think Jessica's haunting you?" A chill ran down Nell's spine. She believed in ghosts, but she'd never dealt with one this close to her own family. What would they do? How would they handle it? What would they say to the kids?

"No, Nellie, not like a damn ghost. Like my wife. Like she pulled herself up out of her grave and walked here. Fucking bleeding and everything, and the *smell...*" He stifled a cough like he was afraid of being heard.

Nell sat on the edge of her bed and wondered what the hell to do. Ghosts she could believe in. It was probably even a natural part of grieving, right? Seeing your dead loved one once or twice more helps you to let go. But the risen dead? Nope. Big fat nope. No logic there, no sense.

"Greg, where're the boys?"

"They're still asleep," he whispered. "I hope to Christ she's gone before they get up, because what the hell can I say to them? How can I explain *that*?"

The sensation of cold grew, creeping up Nell's spine to spread down her shoulders and to her chest. "She's still there?"

"I think so. I can hear her in the kitchen. Let me just..."

"Greg, no, fuck it, stay where you are. If there's someone in the house you need to call the cops, dumbass. Where's your head?"

"I *did* call the cops. I called you." The creak of a door, her brother's ragged breathing into the phone. "*Shit.*" The door slammed close. "Shit, shit, shit, she's still there. She saw me."

"Greg?"

There was shuffling and muffled swearing that sounded far away. Nell scrambled out of bed, her phone pressed to her ear with one hunched shoulder, throwing on the closest jeans and sweatshirt to hand. She scrambled into her snow boots, left sodden and muddy by the front door, and skidded through the dirty slush piled on either side of her driveway. Cranking the engine, she fishtailed onto her silent, suburban street and headed for her brother's house, fifteen minutes across town.

The line went dead before she made it to the car, and every time she called back, she got voicemail. She shivered in the penetrating cold of the car—she hadn't taken the time to warm up the engine, or grab a coat, and it was below 20 degrees. She debated calling the boys—Trevor had his own cell phone and after Jessica's untimely passing, there'd been talk of getting one for Nick. If they were in danger, she could alert them, tell them to leave the house quietly through their bedroom windows.

But what if they were safer where they were? Would getting them up and making noise draw the attention of whoever the hell was in the house? Maybe it was just a crazy person, a confused mental patient who'd wandered into her brother's home and decided she belonged there. Nell knew plenty of women committed violent crimes, but the fact that the intruder was female made her feel a little better about her nephews' safety. It was chilling that Greg hadn't called her back, and wasn't answering his phone now, but maybe he'd forgotten to charge it. Maybe he was even attempting to talk the woman down.

When she pulled up in front of Greg's house, most of

the lights were on. Smoke curled from the chimney into the frigid morning, and the house looked cozy in the predawn, December darkness. Nell made her careful way up the walk, pausing at the front door to listen. She couldn't hear much, only muffled voices, not enough to tell who was speaking or what they were saying. She tried the door, expecting it to be open like it had been every day for the last week, but for once it was locked. She was fumbling for her spare key when the deadbolt clicked. The door swung open, her eldest nephew standing behind it, the remains of a breakfast sandwich in one hand.

"Aunt Nell!" Trevor smiled and stepped back to let her enter, wrapping her in a hug before she could get over the threshold. It was a real hug, the kind he hadn't given her since he'd gotten too big and cool a couple of years ago.

"Everything okay here, kiddo?" she asked, trying to peer past him into the living room.

He let go and smiled again. "It's great. Mom's in the kitchen. Did you come to see her?"

Nell felt that trickle of cold again, her hope of a mistake fading fast. "She's still here, then?" she asked, kicking her snow boots off on the mat by the door.

Trevor's grin widened. "Isn't it awesome?" He headed for the kitchen, almost skipping, but Nell followed slower. The house felt different than it had lately—warmer, more welcoming. She realized it had been cleaned, the shoes, clothes, and electronics that littered the floor on her last visit had been picked up. The empty wine glasses and beer cans were gone, too, and though it wasn't exactly sparkling, things looked a lot better.

As she neared the kitchen she heard happy, boisterous voices talking over one another. She smelled bacon frying but there was something beneath it; a rancid stench, like spoiled meat and copper. She pressed close to the wall, trying to see inside without exposing herself. Then she heard her name spoken.

"Nell?" called Greg. "That you?"

"I told you that, Dad," said Trevor.

Nell took a breath and stepped into the room. Nothing she saw made any sense.

Her brother sat at the kitchen table, a cup of coffee in one hand, a book and note cards spread before him. He was always studying, making notes for a book that Nell doubted would ever materialize, but she hadn't seen him do anything but stare and drink in the last week. He smiled at her, and Trevor, seated at the opposite end, looked up and waved again. Happy enough to give her two greetings.

Nell looked around for Nick and saw him at the stove, leaning on the counter next to it, balanced on one foot and telling what sounded like a very involved story. He was animated and happy, but it was all Nell could do not to run up and snatch him away from the horror he spoke to.

It stood at the kitchen sink, its back to the room, which meant the chunk of missing skull and oozing black goo was visible through strands of clumped, dark hair. Nell's gaze traveled down the figure, catching on but not processing the fact that it wore her sister-in-law's favorite green dress, the one she'd been buried in two days before. It was streaked with mud and other things Nell didn't want to think about. At first, it looked like its head was canted, listening to Nick's story, but Nell realized its neck was broken, the head stuck at an unnatural angle.

Her breath stuttered, coming too fast. She couldn't get enough air, and no words came out of her gasping mouth, but she must have made a sound. The horror began to turn.

"Auntie Nell!" called Nick when he saw her, and launched

himself in her direction. His arms went around her waist and she was left staring at what used to be her brother's wife.

The accident had been bad, an unsecured construction barrel flying from the back of a dump truck and smashing through Jessica's windshield. It killed her instantly, crushing her skull, swelling her brain to the point that the mortician had removed pieces to give her head the right shape. The service had been closed casket—makeup and reconstruction could only do so much, and Jessica's entire face had been smashed back half an inch or so. She looked at Nell now from between drooping eyelids trailing thread, her eyes milky and canted in different directions. Still though, she smiled with torn and ragged lips, more thread pulling loose between them.

"Coffee?" she asked Nell.

Nell didn't know how to answer, but at some point Southern manners kicked in and she found herself at the table with her brother and nephews while the corpse washed dishes. The water ran hot, steaming up the kitchen window, and Nell was mesmerized by the loose, sloughing motion of Jessica's graying hands. She didn't have the heart to say anything to the boys, so demonstrably at peace to have their mother back, but she kept casting glances at Greg. What the fuck must he be thinking? What were any of them thinking? Shit like this didn't happen. All Greg would do was grin at her.

Eventually he excused himself to go shower, and the boys drifted to the living room to play video games. They stayed within sight of the kitchen, and every so often Nell saw them lean back to catch a sight of their mother and grin before going back to their game.

Her heart pounding, sick from the smell of preservatives and rotting flesh, Nell worked up the courage to go to the sink and stand beside the dead woman.

"Jessica?"

The woman shook her head, and a staple worked loose from her scalp, bouncing to the tiles with a tiny ping. "I know what you're going to ask."

Nell stared down at the staple, deep red with blood, a bit of flesh clinging to one end. "And you don't have an answer? To the how, the why, the what the actual *fuck*?"

Jessica laughed, a glottal sound, and another stitch at the corner of her mouth popped free. "The how? No. I've got nothing. And no one's ever known what the *actual* fuck, have they?"

"Then what about the why?" Nell asked, because Jessica seemed to want her to.

The corpse turned off the faucet, pulled her hands from the scalding water and gestured to the house at large. "Why do you think? Have you seen this place? A week is all it took, and I've never been that much of a housekeeper. But not a one of them had clean laundry, I have no idea when the cat was fed last, and there was mold on half the food in the fridge. Nick's out of his asthma medication, Trevor needs family pictures to bring in for class, and Greg hasn't taken his kidney pills even once since I've been gone."

Nell stared at her, brows furrowed, thinking of the state of the house she'd just walked through. "So you came back from the dead...for that?"

Jessica lifted one corner of her mouth in what might have been a rueful smile, if her face cartilage had been intact.

"Someone has to do it," she said, and turned the faucet back on.

Nell watched as Jessica plunged her hands back into the steaming water, one of them degloving in the heat. The corpse didn't seem to notice, humming while she scrubbed a lovely funeral platter.

THE SMALLEST PLACES

You die from the toes up. Did you know that? I mean, not if you die suddenly, I guess. Like if you get hit by a car, you probably start dying wherever the wheels make impact with something vital. I don't know, I'm not an expert on that kind of death. But if you die in bed, like so many people think they want to, it starts with your toes. I learned that when I took a twelve-week training course to get certified as a nurse's assistant. There was a whole section on dealing with death. I'd had experience, losing people, but I'm Southern, so maybe I expected everything to be hushed and vaguely comforting euphemisms. Dumb in retrospect, but I was nineteen, so I forgive myself.

There's a special shroud, too. Apparently they keep it in the bottom of one of your drawers in your hospital room. It makes sense, from a practical standpoint, but ever after that, I checked every hospital room I was ever in, to see if I could find it. That wasn't as many rooms as you might think, because as it turns out, I wasn't cut out for the medical profession. It wasn't because of the death thing, at least I don't think, but it stuck with me. Especially the part about the toes.

I had so many questions. Could you feel it, when the process started? Your living, sparking cells going dark at your lowest extremities. They get cold first, but maybe you don't notice since your feet are always cold these days. But maybe you realize you can't move them. You look down at those innocuous little stubs, twisted in this direction or that, callouses out of control and who knows the last time you had a pedicure. You've just been so tired, these last few years. So you notice your toes, and you feel friendly toward them, so you give them a wiggle. But they don't respond. And at first it's just curious, and you think they must be asleep, but no matter what you do, they won't answer your commands. You start to feel a little panicky, wondering if you're paralyzed. They said that could happen in rare cases, but the rest of your body is working, even if a little sluggish.

So you think maybe it's the medication, making you numb, or even edema. That's another symptom, and you remember how, when you woke up the morning after your C-section, you thought the epidural was still in because you couldn't move your legs. When you said something to the nurse, she looked confused, then she lifted the sheet covering your legs and you screamed. You weren't expecting it, the swelling that made them elephantine, almost immobile, but it went away in time, so maybe that's what's going on here. So you lift the sheet, but your legs look like they always have, a little thick but nothing out of the ordinary.

Can you see the difference in your toes? When you look again, do they seem any different? Does rigor set in early, or is it just that indefinable difference in appearance that separates dead flesh from live? And if you *can* see it, are you horrified, watching inexorable death creep up your body? Or are you peaceful? Aren't you supposed to die in your sleep?

But you're not sleeping, you're awake, and how could you be peaceful? You knew this was coming, it's not a surprise, but in a way it's always a surprise. You thought you'd have a little more time, Drew and Angie and the kids are coming this afternoon and you were sure you'd have that, at least. You've heard of people fighting to stick around, hanging on to make it through Christmas or whatever. All you want is a few more hours, and surely you can fight that hard. You've always been a fighter, so you start.

But what if you do manage to stop the process somehow, the reaper's job only partway through? Will your toes, and now your calves, come back to you, or have they already crossed over? Are they ghost toes, just waiting for you to catch up?

You're not sure how this kind of fight is supposed to go. You can't visualize your enemy, and anyway you don't want to think of death as your enemy. That would upset the delicate balance of acceptance you've cultivated. You're at peace with dying, because you have to be. For Drew's sake, and the kids. Your grand babies, not babies anymore but still too young to be watching this happen. You wonder if instead of fighting you should try letting go to spare them this. What if they were to walk in with your death half done? What might that do to their tender psyches?

It turns out you're as vague on the process of letting go as you are of fighting. You were always bad at meditation, clearing your mind and relaxing. You cleared your mind with exercise, back when you were fit enough, and with hard work long after you should have. But you can't get out of this bed, and the call button, wrapped around the bed rail, has fallen where you cannot reach. You try to call out but your voice is thin, the breath behind it weak and flimsy. You banish that and concentrate again on fighting.

How do you fight? You strike back, right? You have no weapons, so instead you push. You press against the slow creep turning your body into unresponsive concrete. It's reached your knee caps now, so that's where you start, picturing yourself standing Gandalf-style on the bridge of your thighs, palms pressed outward against death. You push as hard as you can against it, one woman holding back a tidal wave, but a strange *whoosh* happens and you find yourself squashed against your own sternum. Before you, the ooze of finality has crossed and claimed most of your torso without you even seeing. Was that because you were unconscious? Or did that push do it? Did you speed your own ticking clock?

Either way, it doesn't seem to be reversible, and you're afraid of what will happen when it covers the rest of your lungs. Already it's hard to draw breath, and as a lifelong asthmatic, you recoil from the idea of a slow suffocation.

But it's coming for you. It's not stopping, and whoever these other folks were, the ones who made it to one last holiday or anniversary or birthday, it's not you. You won't make it out of this room alive. You don't remember when I became you, but that's where we are, because second person is hard to pull off, but not as hard as watching yourself die.

You stare it down, this wave of your own demise, watching the changing of your flesh into stone. It's still coming, and soon you'll be trapped in your head, if you can't find a way out.

Out. Is that it? Is that what you're supposed to be doing, to miss experiencing this execution? Did you miss check out time and now you're caught in the cleaner's sweep? Where's the white light? The out of body experience? No more thought of sticking around, you just don't want to be there when death reaches you.

But you see nothing, hear nothing that can help you. You're alone, and the cold is getting close. Where to go? Your gaze bounces as much as it can, searching for the exit sign.

There. To your right, a forgotten corner. You have just enough room to slide past the encroaching dark: it hasn't found this place yet. There's a corridor in front of you, and you take it. You don't want to be there to see the end.

The farther you travel, the more it seems as though something at the end of this place is calling you. Did you leave your body after all? Is this your way to the other side? But no. You arrive, after a brief narrowing, in a sort of wide entryway, with five paths leading from it. It feels warm here, and familiar. You reach out to touch the walls of this place, and find tenderness. It seems to touch you back, to pull you into an embrace, and you stretch out to fill your new space. You reach through the five paths and touch the rough end of each one.

More warmth, and you're in a full body hug, now. Not from this place, because you *are* this place now, and it is you. You're being held by someone who loves you, who you love, and they are crying. You could reassure them, tell them it's not goodbye, but your voice is gone along with the rest of you, so all you can do is squeeze back.

You *have* been called home. It's not a destination you expected, but it is one you remember well. You have done good and loving work from this home, back when it was only a small part of you. Now it *is* you, and peace has returned to your heart. It may not last forever, but it's here for now, and there is much to do. So you stretch, and you move, and you feel your way as you ponder how best to separate yourself from what you used to be. How to prune what has died so you may go on as what you have become, for however long you're here. You may have a hard time blending in this form, but you'll find a way. Maybe even make yourself useful, join a household of sorts. The kind of kooks who are so creepy themselves, you'll feel right at home.

That would be nice.

ABOUT THE AUTHOR

Laurel Hightower grew up in Lexington, Kentucky, and after forays to California and Tennessee, has returned home to horse country. She's a fan of true life ghost stories, horror movies, and good bourbon. She is the author of *Whispers In The Dark*, *Crossroads*, and *Below*, and has more than a dozen short story credits to her name, including publications through Burial Day Press, Cemetery Gates, Brigid's Gate, Dead Sea Press, Brian Keene's Patreon, and Dark Hart Books. Crossroads was the recipient of an Independent Audiobook Award in 2020 in the category of Best Horror, as well as the This is Horror Best Novella Award for 2020. She has also co-edited three anthologies: *We Are Wolves*, a charity anthology released in 2020 by Burial Day Press, *The Dead Inside*, an anthology of identity horror released in 2022 by Dark Dispatch, and *Shattered & Splintered*, a charity anthology released in 2022 to benefit the Glen Haven Area Volunteer Fire Department, who saved the historic Stanley Hotel from wildfires in 2020. *Every Woman Knows This* is her first collection.

CONTENT
WARNINGS

Attempted sexual assault:
Every Woman Knows This
One of those Faces

Implied sexual assault:
One of Those Faces
Though Your Heart is Breaking

Physical abuse/Relationship abuse:
One of Those Faces

Cancer:
Vignettes of Womanhood: Scar Tissue

Childbirth:
The Midwife

Fertility:
The Little Head

Miscarriage implied:
Though Your Heart is Breaking

Depression/Post-partum depression:
Starman

Child abuse:
Starman

Body dysmorphia:
The Little Head

Experience of death explored:
The Smallest Places